ALREADY COLD

(A Laura Frost Suspense Thriller—Book Eleven)

BLAKE PIERCE

Blake Pierce

Blake Pierce is the USA Today bestselling author of the RILEY PAGE mystery series, which includes seventeen books. Blake Pierce is also the author of the MACKENZIE WHITE mystery series, comprising fourteen books; of the AVERY BLACK mystery series, comprising six books; of the KERI LOCKE mystery series, comprising five books; of the MAKING OF RILEY PAIGE mystery series, comprising six books; of the KATE WISE mystery series, comprising seven books; of the CHLOE FINE psychological suspense mystery, comprising six books; of the JESSIE HUNT psychological suspense thriller series, comprising twenty six books; of the AU PAIR psychological suspense thriller series, comprising three books; of the ZOE PRIME mystery series, comprising six books; of the ADELE SHARP mystery series, comprising sixteen books, of the EUROPEAN VOYAGE cozy mystery series, comprising six books; of the LAURA FROST FBI suspense thriller, comprising eleven books; of the ELLA DARK FBI suspense thriller, comprising fourteen books (and counting); of the A YEAR IN EUROPE cozy mystery series, comprising nine books, of the AVA GOLD mystery series, comprising six books; of the RACHEL GIFT mystery series, comprising ten books (and counting); of the VALERIE LAW mystery series, comprising nine books (and counting); of the PAIGE KING mystery series, comprising eight books (and counting); of the MAY MOORE mystery series, comprising eleven books (and counting); the CORA SHIELDS mystery series, comprising five books (and counting); of the NICKY LYONS mystery series, comprising seven books (and counting), of the CAMI LARK mystery series, comprising five books (and counting), of the AMBER YOUNG mystery series, comprising five books (and counting), and of the new DAISY FORTUNE mystery series, comprising five books (and counting).

An avid reader and lifelong fan of the mystery and thriller genres, Blake loves to hear from you, so please feel free to visit www.blakepierceauthor.com to learn more and stay in touch.

ISBN: 978-1-0943-8070-4

BOOKS BY BLAKE PIERCE

DAISY FORTUNE MYSTERY SERIES
NEED YOU (Book #1)
CLAIM YOU (Book #2)
CRAVE YOU (Book #3)
CHOOSE YOU (Book #4)
CHASE YOU (Book #5)

AMBER YOUNG MYSTERY SERIES
ABSENT PITY (Book #1)
ABSENT REMORSE (Book #2)
ABSENT FEELING (Book #3)
ABSENT MERCY (Book #4)
ABSENT REASON (Book #5)

CAMI LARK MYSTERY SERIES
JUST ME (Book #1)
JUST OUTSIDE (Book #2)
JUST RIGHT (Book #3)
JUST FORGET (Book #4)
JUST ONCE (Book #5)

NICKY LYONS MYSTERY SERIES
ALL MINE (Book #1)
ALL HIS (Book #2)
ALL HE SEES (Book #3)
ALL ALONE (Book #4)
ALL FOR ONE (Book #5)
ALL HE TAKES (Book #6)
ALL FOR ME (Book #7)

CORA SHIELDS MYSTERY SERIES
UNDONE (Book #1)
UNWANTED (Book #2)
UNHINGED (Book #3)
UNSAID (Book #4)
UNGLUED (Book #5)

MAY MOORE SUSPENSE THRILLER
NEVER RUN (Book #1)
NEVER TELL (Book #2)
NEVER LIVE (Book #3)
NEVER HIDE (Book #4)
NEVER FORGIVE (Book #5)
NEVER AGAIN (Book #6)
NEVER LOOK BACK (Book #7)
NEVER FORGET (Book #8)
NEVER LET GO (Book #9)
NEVER PRETEND (Book #10)
NEVER HESITATE (Book #11)

PAIGE KING MYSTERY SERIES
THE GIRL HE PINED (Book #1)
THE GIRL HE CHOSE (Book #2)
THE GIRL HE TOOK (Book #3)
THE GIRL HE WISHED (Book #4)
THE GIRL HE CROWNED (Book #5)
THE GIRL HE WATCHED (Book #6)
THE GIRL HE WANTED (Book #7)
THE GIRL HE CLAIMED (Book #8)

VALERIE LAW MYSTERY SERIES
NO MERCY (Book #1)
NO PITY (Book #2)
NO FEAR (Book #3)
NO SLEEP (Book #4)
NO QUARTER (Book #5)
NO CHANCE (Book #6)
NO REFUGE (Book #7)
NO GRACE (Book #8)
NO ESCAPE (Book #9)

RACHEL GIFT MYSTERY SERIES
HER LAST WISH (Book #1)
HER LAST CHANCE (Book #2)
HER LAST HOPE (Book #3)
HER LAST FEAR (Book #4)
HER LAST CHOICE (Book #5)
HER LAST BREATH (Book #6)

HER LAST MISTAKE (Book #7)
HER LAST DESIRE (Book #8)
HER LAST REGRET (Book #9)
HER LAST HOUR (Book #10)

AVA GOLD MYSTERY SERIES
CITY OF PREY (Book #1)
CITY OF FEAR (Book #2)
CITY OF BONES (Book #3)
CITY OF GHOSTS (Book #4)
CITY OF DEATH (Book #5)
CITY OF VICE (Book #6)

A YEAR IN EUROPE
A MURDER IN PARIS (Book #1)
DEATH IN FLORENCE (Book #2)
VENGEANCE IN VIENNA (Book #3)
A FATALITY IN SPAIN (Book #4)

ELLA DARK FBI SUSPENSE THRILLER
GIRL, ALONE (Book #1)
GIRL, TAKEN (Book #2)
GIRL, HUNTED (Book #3)
GIRL, SILENCED (Book #4)
GIRL, VANISHED (Book 5)
GIRL ERASED (Book #6)
GIRL, FORSAKEN (Book #7)
GIRL, TRAPPED (Book #8)
GIRL, EXPENDABLE (Book #9)
GIRL, ESCAPED (Book #10)
GIRL, HIS (Book #11)
GIRL, LURED (Book #12)
GIRL, MISSING (Book #13)
GIRL, UNKNOWN (Book #14)

LAURA FROST FBI SUSPENSE THRILLER
ALREADY GONE (Book #1)
ALREADY SEEN (Book #2)
ALREADY TRAPPED (Book #3)
ALREADY MISSING (Book #4)
ALREADY DEAD (Book #5)

ALREADY TAKEN (Book #6)
ALREADY CHOSEN (Book #7)
ALREADY LOST (Book #8)
ALREADY HIS (Book #9)
ALREADY LURED (Book #10)
ALREADY COLD (Book #11)

EUROPEAN VOYAGE COZY MYSTERY SERIES
MURDER (AND BAKLAVA) (Book #1)
DEATH (AND APPLE STRUDEL) (Book #2)
CRIME (AND LAGER) (Book #3)
MISFORTUNE (AND GOUDA) (Book #4)
CALAMITY (AND A DANISH) (Book #5)
MAYHEM (AND HERRING) (Book #6)

ADELE SHARP MYSTERY SERIES
LEFT TO DIE (Book #1)
LEFT TO RUN (Book #2)
LEFT TO HIDE (Book #3)
LEFT TO KILL (Book #4)
LEFT TO MURDER (Book #5)
LEFT TO ENVY (Book #6)
LEFT TO LAPSE (Book #7)
LEFT TO VANISH (Book #8)
LEFT TO HUNT (Book #9)
LEFT TO FEAR (Book #10)
LEFT TO PREY (Book #11)
LEFT TO LURE (Book #12)
LEFT TO CRAVE (Book #13)
LEFT TO LOATHE (Book #14)
LEFT TO HARM (Book #15)
LEFT TO RUIN (Book #16)

THE AU PAIR SERIES
ALMOST GONE (Book#1)
ALMOST LOST (Book #2)
ALMOST DEAD (Book #3)

ZOE PRIME MYSTERY SERIES
FACE OF DEATH (Book#1)
FACE OF MURDER (Book #2)

FACE OF FEAR (Book #3)
FACE OF MADNESS (Book #4)
FACE OF FURY (Book #5)
FACE OF DARKNESS (Book #6)

A JESSIE HUNT PSYCHOLOGICAL SUSPENSE SERIES
THE PERFECT WIFE (Book #1)
THE PERFECT BLOCK (Book #2)
THE PERFECT HOUSE (Book #3)
THE PERFECT SMILE (Book #4)
THE PERFECT LIE (Book #5)
THE PERFECT LOOK (Book #6)
THE PERFECT AFFAIR (Book #7)
THE PERFECT ALIBI (Book #8)
THE PERFECT NEIGHBOR (Book #9)
THE PERFECT DISGUISE (Book #10)
THE PERFECT SECRET (Book #11)
THE PERFECT FAÇADE (Book #12)
THE PERFECT IMPRESSION (Book #13)
THE PERFECT DECEIT (Book #14)
THE PERFECT MISTRESS (Book #15)
THE PERFECT IMAGE (Book #16)
THE PERFECT VEIL (Book #17)
THE PERFECT INDISCRETION (Book #18)
THE PERFECT RUMOR (Book #19)
THE PERFECT COUPLE (Book #20)
THE PERFECT MURDER (Book #21)
THE PERFECT HUSBAND (Book #22)
THE PERFECT SCANDAL (Book #23)
THE PERFECT MASK (Book #24)
THE PERFECT RUSE (Book #25)
THE PERFECT VENEER (Book #26)

CHLOE FINE PSYCHOLOGICAL SUSPENSE SERIES
NEXT DOOR (Book #1)
A NEIGHBOR'S LIE (Book #2)
CUL DE SAC (Book #3)
SILENT NEIGHBOR (Book #4)
HOMECOMING (Book #5)
TINTED WINDOWS (Book #6)

KATE WISE MYSTERY SERIES

IF SHE KNEW (Book #1)

IF SHE SAW (Book #2)

IF SHE RAN (Book #3)

IF SHE HID (Book #4)

IF SHE FLED (Book #5)

IF SHE FEARED (Book #6)

IF SHE HEARD (Book #7)

THE MAKING OF RILEY PAIGE SERIES

WATCHING (Book #1)

WAITING (Book #2)

LURING (Book #3)

TAKING (Book #4)

STALKING (Book #5)

KILLING (Book #6)

RILEY PAIGE MYSTERY SERIES

ONCE GONE (Book #1)

ONCE TAKEN (Book #2)

ONCE CRAVED (Book #3)

ONCE LURED (Book #4)

ONCE HUNTED (Book #5)

ONCE PINED (Book #6)

ONCE FORSAKEN (Book #7)

ONCE COLD (Book #8)

ONCE STALKED (Book #9)

ONCE LOST (Book #10)

ONCE BURIED (Book #11)

ONCE BOUND (Book #12)

ONCE TRAPPED (Book #13)

ONCE DORMANT (Book #14)

ONCE SHUNNED (Book #15)

ONCE MISSED (Book #16)

ONCE CHOSEN (Book #17)

MACKENZIE WHITE MYSTERY SERIES

BEFORE HE KILLS (Book #1)

BEFORE HE SEES (Book #2)

BEFORE HE COVETS (Book #3)

BEFORE HE TAKES (Book #4)

BEFORE HE NEEDS (Book #5)
BEFORE HE FEELS (Book #6)
BEFORE HE SINS (Book #7)
BEFORE HE HUNTS (Book #8)
BEFORE HE PREYS (Book #9)
BEFORE HE LONGS (Book #10)
BEFORE HE LAPSES (Book #11)
BEFORE HE ENVIES (Book #12)
BEFORE HE STALKS (Book #13)
BEFORE HE HARMS (Book #14)

AVERY BLACK MYSTERY SERIES
CAUSE TO KILL (Book #1)
CAUSE TO RUN (Book #2)
CAUSE TO HIDE (Book #3)
CAUSE TO FEAR (Book #4)
CAUSE TO SAVE (Book #5)
CAUSE TO DREAD (Book #6)

KERI LOCKE MYSTERY SERIES
A TRACE OF DEATH (Book #1)
A TRACE OF MURDER (Book #2)
A TRACE OF VICE (Book #3)
A TRACE OF CRIME (Book #4)
A TRACE OF HOPE (Book #5)

CHAPTER ONE

Joy stumbled a little to the side and considered the idea that maybe that last drink had been one too many.

She blinked her eyes and tried to focus. The cold night air was helping some, but not enough. She still felt way too drunk. She'd been aiming for tipsy and somehow managed to sail right over it to the wrong side. Not a smart idea when she had a long walk home. The kind of long walk she wouldn't normally consider if she hadn't been drinking too much to drive back.

A long walk home around the very outskirts of town that passed right by the woods, no less.

Joy cleared her throat out loud, just for something to hear, and dragged her thin jacket tighter around her shoulders.

A car passed by fast, the headlights sweeping over and past her, and Joy found herself stumbling closer to the trees – afraid for a moment that she would sway into the path of the car if she wasn't careful.

This wasn't a fun walk at the best of times. Her feet were numbed by the alcohol and so she couldn't quite yet feel the pain she logically knew her high heels must be inflicting, but she would soon. As soon as she sobered up just a little bit more. And there was still far to go, past the woods and on down a few blocks.

Only one way through, though, and that was onwards.

Joy clattered her heels against the sidewalk as she attempted to speed up, trying to tell herself she would never do this again but equally wondering if she was even going to remember that thought in the morning.

There was a crunch somewhere behind her – a shoe coming down on a loose pebble.

Joy glanced over her shoulder, her long, heavy hair moving with her, and saw a man. At least, she assumed it was a man. He was walking behind her, but he was wearing a big dark coat and a hat, and she couldn't make out anything more than that.

Joy looked ahead and tried to focus on going forward, trying desperately not to sway on her feet even though she knew she already was. If she went too fast, she felt like she was going to fall over or stumble into one of the trees on her left. She was walking in and out of the circles of illumination under streetlights, plunging into darkness between them, and the glare of the lights made it almost impossible to see anything past the nearest line of trees.

She glanced back over her shoulder again.

He was getting closer.

Joy wasn't sure she could speed up anymore, not in these heels and not with this drink running through her veins – even though she was already starting to feel a little more sober.

Which was kind of the problem, because now her feet were hurting and she felt the cold, and she was starting to feel a lot more scared than brave.

She glanced ahead. There was a row of stores on the other side of the road, Mickey's and a few other places, but they were all dark. Empty. The lights off, no one home. There was no one there to help her. And past them, she knew from experience, there wasn't much of anything for a bit. No cars had gone past since that last one. It could be a while before another one came.

She could be on her own with this man for long enough for him to do anything to her, before another witness came by, if she didn't try to get away.

Joy glanced back again and her heart thudded painfully against her chest. He was closer still. He had his hands shoved in his pockets as if he was hiding something, and he was looking right at her.

Right at her.

Joy wasn't going to take any chances. She looked ahead again and then did the only thing she could think of.

She plunged off the path and into the woods, the darkness quickly swallowing her up as she moved out of the range of the streetlights, so thick she couldn't see where she was putting her feet. She stumbled a few times, grabbing onto tree trunks to keep herself upright, her heels sinking slightly into soft patches of the ground.

Joy turned to look over her shoulder and stopped. She turned around fully to watch. The man in the black coat – she could still see him through the trunks of the trees. He was right under one of the streetlights. Walking.

Walking forward along the path as though nothing had happened.

Joy let out a ragged breath, then covered her mouth with a relieved gasp. He wasn't coming after her, after all. She'd been afraid for no reason.

He wasn't following her at all.

There was a crack in the trees near her, and Joy turned her head sharply in that direction. It was dark under the foliage, but somehow she glimpsed him. Another man. Another man in dark clothing.

And this one…

This one was running right at her with something in his hand, and Joy wasn't going to wait around to find out what it was.

She turned and ran at full speed away from him, deeper into the woods, feeling instinctively that this time was the real thing. She had to put as much distance between the two of them as possible. She felt one of her heels come loose and let it go, kicking her other foot on the next step to get rid of that one too so she would be even. The ground was alternating hard and soft under her bare feet, bouncy moss that seemed to propel her forward but roots and sharp twigs scratching at her and threatening to make her fall. She had never felt more sober in her life.

Joy burst out of the tree line into an open space, a clearing, the sky framed by branches all around. There was a sort of cabin, she supposed, built there – it looked old and was only large enough for a single room, but it was there. She surged towards it, thinking it might be shelter. She reached the door and pounded on it, but –

He was right behind her.

She managed to dart to the side just before he was upon her, her legs propelling her forward in an ungainly and desperate dash that had her arms flailing to the sides for balance. She threw herself back towards the trees –

She'd hit something with her foot, maybe another tree root, but the next thing she knew she was flying through the air. She landed heavy, coming down on her side, the air whooshing out of her at the impact. She only had time to turn slightly before he was upon her – over her – so close she could see his teeth bared in a grin.

So close she had no time, no time at all – Joy opened her mouth to scream as he trapped her arms with his legs, pinning her in place – his hands came down towards her and she was powerless to do a thing but watch…

And Joy knew it was over.

The last thought in her mind was that drink, that one more drink she decided to have, and the car sitting, waiting for her so that she could have driven home in safety--if she’d stopped before that drink.

CHAPTER TWO

Laura sat bolt upright in bed, drenched in sweat. She wasn't even sure if she had screamed, but if she had, there was no one else in the apartment to hear it. She fought for breath for a moment until she could get herself back under control, holding her head in her hands.

What was that?

A vision, she was sure of it. But it had been so real, so visceral. It was like she was actually there, and not only that, but she was there *as the woman who had been attacked.* Not like she was a camera following her, or even a camera looking through her eyes. She felt like she was the woman herself. She understood what she was thinking, felt her emotions, even felt the stabs of pain in the soles of her feet.

Laura had bad dreams before. She'd even had vision dreams. But this…

It was so much more, so much stronger than anything she'd ever seen.

It was like knowing Zach, the only other psychic she had ever met, had been a serious blessing. At first, their proximity to one another had caused both of their abilities to act up and go haywire, almost disappearing at points, but now… it was like it had come back better than ever before.

Almost like being close to another psychic had allowed her abilities to evolve and grow, maybe even to learn from his. Laura didn't know how it worked. She never had known, which was always part of the problem. But something had happened – and now she could see better than ever.

Her head was pounding, an unfortunate side effect which always came with her visions. Laura felt the pressure on her neck, on the other woman's neck, putting up her hands to touch the place where it had been. She was sure she had felt herself being strangled like it was real. It had happened to her recently, after all. The red marks had faded in the month or so since, but…

Laura scrambled out of bed and went to her bathroom, turning on the light. She stared at herself in the mirror above the sink. Same blonde ponytail, same blue eyes that she expected. But her neck was clear, the skin pale and white, no trace of a red mark on it. It was just a vision. The feeling was just… a ghost.

A ghost of something that hadn't yet happened.

And that was the most important point – because Laura had been given a chance to see the future, and she needed to do something to make sure it never came to pass.

She walked out into her small living room, sitting down on the battered second-hand sofa that had been all she could afford after the divorce. She checked the time on her cell phone: It was a little after three in the morning.

But getting woken up at all hours of the night, or interrupted at all hours of the day, for a case – that was the job. That was being an FBI agent. And surely, surely, when a life was at stake… an agent wouldn't mind.

Laura quit trying to reason with herself and dialed Nate's number anyway, knowing she needed her partner by her side before she even attempted to do anything about what she had seen.

The line rang three times before he answered. "Laura? We have a case?"

"Not quite," Laura said. She considered it. "But maybe."

"What?" Nate's voice was a little off, somewhat muffled by sleep, and she heard him shift in bed to look at the clock. "Laura, it's three in the morning. I need you to make more sense than that."

"I saw something," Laura said, cutting right to the chase. "It's not an official case. But it's a murder. We have to stop it."

"Okay." Nate sounded a lot more alert immediately, like he'd sat up and woken up. "What do you want me to do?"

"Meet me," Laura said. "Help me figure it out."

"I'll be there in fifteen," Nate said, and hung up.

***

"Hey," Laura said, throwing the door open wide and leaning out to glance up and down the hall. She couldn't see or hear any movement from her neighbors, which was good. If any of them had been woken up by Nate knocking on her door at half past three in the morning, they wouldn't be happy with her.

"Hi," Nate said in a hushed voice. He was tall and well-built enough to almost fill the frame of her door. She stepped aside and he moved into the apartment past her, quickly glancing around at her home. It was not often that either of them visited one another's living spaces.

"Thanks for coming over," Laura said. She felt a rush of something unfamiliar – like gratitude and relief and something even lighter all rolled up together. She'd never been able to do this before. A few short months ago, no one else in the world had known about her ability. Now that she had told Nate, and he had accepted and embraced her visions, she had someone she could call on when she saw something important. It was an incredible feeling.

"Of course," Nate replied easily. He found his way to the sofa – not difficult, given that the kitchen and living room were open plan and the entrance opened right in to them – and sank onto it. "You said there's a life to save, so let's save it."

Laura grinned, dropping down next to him. "Okay. I saw a vision of a woman being stalked and then attacked in the middle of the woods, late at night."

Nate frowned. "Not a lot to go on there."

"No, not a lot," Laura said. "But I did have some clues. The weather was cold, and I had a huge headache when I woke up, so I figure it's happening soon."

"Makes sense," Nate said. "Unless she's in a place where February is hot."

"Then why would I have a vision about her?" Laura asked.

"I don't know," Nate shrugged. "It's probably happening soon. Go on."

"The location she was going to looked like a small cabin of some kind, like a one-room kind of place, in the middle of a clearing past the woods, but it wasn't far from the main road," Laura continued. "She ran a good distance, far enough to not hear cars anymore, but it was still a distance she could run on foot – in bare feet, actually."

"Okay." Nate frowned. "But… even if we were to limit the search radius to this state alone, surely we'd probably find a lot of places like that."

"Correct," Laura said, then held up a finger. "That's where it gets interesting."

"You're enjoying this," Nate said, with a light smile.

"Of course, I am," Laura chuckled. Even though the situation was obviously serious, this was what she enjoyed most in life: getting a clue and figuring out what it meant so that she could save a life. When successfully solving a puzzle not only made you feel smart, but also stopped a killer, it was the ultimate dopamine rush. "Okay. I saw a row of stores in the vision. It was dark, all the lights were switched off because they were closed, but I was able to get the name of the nearest one. Mickey's."

Nate looked at her hard. "Mickey's."

"Yes," Laura nodded.

"And how many places in the United States, let alone the world, do you think are called Mickey's?"

"Oh, hundreds," Laura said. She tilted her head, considering it. "If not thousands, probably."

Nate sighed. "I take it from your unworried tone that you've figured out a way to get around that problem."

"Sort of," Laura said. "I haven't acted on it yet, but I was thinking about it as I was waiting for you, and I think the only way we can get a good lead on it is to speak to Dean."

"Dean?" Nate frowned, then his expression cleared a little – but only to look slightly disappointed. "Dean Marsters?"

"Yeah." Laura frowned at his look. "What's wrong with that?"

Nate shook his head. "Nothing."

"What?" Laura pushed.

"Well, you could ask any other person from the tech department, you know," Nate said.

"No, I can't," Laura replied. "It's too dangerous. No one else will do it for me and keep it quiet."

"Why does it need to be quiet?"

"Because…" Laura looked at him wide-eyed. "Well, we can't tell anyone else about this case. We can't admit how I know about it."

"Wait, you don't want to tell Rondelle we're investigating this?" Nate asked, shaking his head.

"You didn't imagine we could, really, did you?" Laura was incredulous. "Nate, think about it. What's the first thing he would ask?"

Nate paused. When he answered, it was with reluctance. "Where the lead came from."

"Right! So, you see the problem."

Nate nodded. "I do. It's just… this feels weird. Going… what, freelance?"

"I know," Laura said. "But, if this is what we need to do in order to save a life, then I've made my peace with it. Is that okay with you?"

Nate sighed deeply, but nodded again. "I guess it has to be. You're right. Saving a life is more important than following protocol."

"Now we've established that, circling back around to my earlier point – Dean will do a search for me and keep it quiet. He's good like that."

"Don't you see how that makes it worse?"

Laura blinked at him. "Why?"

Nate rolled his eyes. "He has a massive crush on you, Laura. Like, huge."

"No, he doesn't," Laura immediately refuted. "He's just a good guy. We get on well, so he helps me out with stuff. He knows that if I get good results, he'll be mentioned in the briefing after the case and he'll get a better chance of a promotion."

"Sure," Nate said drily. "That's it. Laura, you're basically leading him on."

"How am I leading him on? We've never even been on a date. He's never even *asked* me on a date," Laura said. She sighed and waved her hands between them, trying to physically clear the topic out of the way. "Look, it doesn't matter. We can do as much research ourselves as we can for now, and then when the office opens in the morning, I'll be able to give him a call if we still need help."

Nate groaned. "Fine," he said. "But I'm only okay with this because you haven't been wrong yet, and I don't want someone to die when I could have helped stop it."

"Noted," Laura said. "That's why I'm doing this, too. So, I guess the first thing we need to do is start going through every place called Mickey's that's near some woodland."

Nate lifted his hands into the air. "That's going to take so long! Haven't you got anything else to narrow it down by?"

"Yes, but we can't use it yet," Laura said. "I saw a car drive past. I saw the license plate. But we're going to need to access the DMV system for that, and Dean's our best help there, too."

"Fine." Nate scrubbed his hands across his face, then pulled out his cell phone. "I wish I had a computer for this."

"Use my laptop, then," Laura suggested, grabbing it from the coffee table. "I'll use my cell. I don't mind if it's slow. So long as we get there."

Nate nodded, firing the machine up and already focusing on the task at hand. "I'll take D.C. first," he said. "In case it's close by."

"I'll go for Washington state, in case it's not," Laura said, with a half-smile.

They got to work in silence. Laura zoomed her map into the Washington state area and then searched for Mickey's, biting her lip at the sheer number of results that came up but staying quiet. She didn't want to admit to Nate that she thought this was going to be stupidly hard, too. But what choice did they have? The quicker they found out where the murder was going to take place, the better. It was probably three hours before Dean would be at his desk, if not four. In that time, they might even find it.

She scanned each result's position, clicking on the ones that came up with a couple of other buildings nearby and an area of woodland on the side. One by one, she checked out the street view and ruled them out.

"Any of these strike you as familiar?" Nate asked. He clicked through five or six tabs he had opened up, each with an image of the front of the place – stores and cafés and diners.

"None of those yet," Laura said. "Keep going."

Nate sighed and settled deeper into the couch. "You realize this could take us all week?"

"We just need to keep going until Dean gets into work, remember," Laura said. As a safety measure, she fired off a quick text message to the FBI tech in question, asking him to respond when he was at his desk. The second it was possible to do the search, they would be ready.

And in the meantime, Laura would spend every available second that she had to see if they could get to the solution faster – and maybe find the location before it was too late.

CHAPTER THREE

Laura looked at her buzzing phone and grabbed it from the coffee table, looking at Nate. "Time," she said. "Dean's in. He said I can call him whenever I'm ready."

Nate let his head fall against the back of the sofa, the curve of the cushions supporting his neck. "Fine," he said, setting the laptop aside. "I give up. Call in the cavalry. He must be able to narrow it down a lot faster than this."

"Great," Laura said, quickly hitting the call button next to Dean's name and putting it to her ear.

"Yeah?" Dean said, in his normal manner, always refusing to answer the phone with a proper Bureau greeting as he was supposed to. Or maybe he just saw Laura's caller ID and always liked to make it seem like they were just picking up from their last conversation, even though they could go for weeks without talking.

"Dean!" Laura exclaimed. "I need a hand finding a location."

"Alright. What's the case?" Dean asked. Most of the time, in order to assign billing and man hours correctly, techs and other support staff within the FBI had to enter a case number to be able to log their work. It was part of the system that made it difficult to do anything you weren't supposed to… but not impossible.

"No official case," Laura said. "This is a special one. We got a tip-off about someone hanging around there and we need to check it out – it could be related to a murder. We just don't have a case yet until we verify everything."

"Laura," Dean said, in a sing-song voice. "Is that code for, you haven't asked the boss yet?"

"Well, I can't ask him until I know whether it's worth checking out," Laura reasoned.

"Of course," Dean said. "Well, okay. Tell me what you've got. But you're going to owe me a burger."

"I'll send you something to the office," Laura said quickly, remembering Nate's earlier words. If that was Dean's subtle way of trying to get her to go out on a date with him, she needed to head the idea off now. At least if she was clear, there wouldn't be any accusations that she was taking advantage of him. "I have a car registration, and I need to know where it's from. It was seen driving along the road opposite a certain store."

"Why don't you just look up the store name?"

"It was too generic," Laura explained. "Mickey's. We looked it up. There are thousands of places called that in the U.S. alone. We presume the case is national, and probably more local if anything else, but we haven't been able to narrow down the field enough."

Dean seemed to hesitate. "How did you get this information?" he asked. "If it was seen, then surely you can just ask the witness where they were."

Laura hadn't thought of that. She racked her brain as fast as she could, her mouth opening to give the excuse before she could really finish thinking it through. "It was a video," she said. "We were sent a video, and the metadata has been wiped clean."

"Can I see it?"

"No," Laura said, cursing herself and having to think fast again. Why was she giving him answers that just invited more questions? "It was sent to us via a secure link and since we watched it, it's been wiped."

"Oh," Dean said. "Well, just give me the link and I can see if I can do any kind of recovery – or find out where the IP address was based."

"If it's okay, we'd rather focus on the location in the video," Laura said, closing her eyes and hoping the nightmare would stop.

"Okay, fine, I'll do what I can," Dean said. "So, give me the rest. We have Mickey's, we have a car registration – anything else?"

"Opposite the Mickey's is a stretch of wooded area," Laura said. "Down through the way a bit, there's a cabin or hut or something based in a clearing in the trees."

"Great," Dean said. She could hear the sound of typing in the background. "And that vehicle registration?"

Laura recited it to him from memory. "Is that enough information? Oh, there were a couple of other buildings next to Mickey's, but it wasn't possible to make out what they were."

"I'll see what I can do," Dean said. "Okay, I already have the registration details up. Looks like it's registered in Maryland."

"Maryland," Laura said out loud, for Nate's benefit. "God, we were looking in D.C.! We were so close."

"Okay, I have it."

"What?"

"I have the location."

Laura blinked. "Already?"

"It's a very precise set of principles," Dean said. "A place called Mickey's opposite woodland with a neighboring building in Maryland. Plus, it's actually not far from the town where the car is registered. You want the address?"

"Yes, absolutely," Laura said, shaking her head at Nate in surprised wonder. "Can you send it to me in a text? We'll get right over there."

"Sure thing," Dean said. "Don't forget my burger!"

"Thanks, Dean!" Laura said, ending the call. "He's found it!"

"Just like that," Nate said drily.

"Yes, he -" Laura stopped as she realized he was making fun of her. "Well, I didn't expect him to get it that fast."

"I heard," Nate said. "I also heard you being such a bad liar; I don't know how I ever actually believed your excuses for your visions."

"Well, you didn't," Laura pointed out. "That's why you were suspicious in the first place."

"Maybe I should start giving the excuses from now on," Nate said with a smirk. "Before you get us into even deeper trouble."

"We should call in," Laura said, looking at the clock on the car's dashboard.

"You want to report it? We're not even there yet," Nate argued. "There's still a couple of minutes to go on the route."

"Not call *it* in," Laura said. She kept an eye on the GPS and the road ahead at the same time. It was a straight path from here to the destination, but she wanted to stay alert in case it was off. "I mean call in and tell them we won't be in the office today."

"Good shout." Nate paused with his hand on his cell phone. "What should I tell them as an excuse?"

"We're following a lead from an informant," Laura said. "Why not? They don't have to know what it is yet. If it comes to nothing, that's what we'll say. It was nothing."

"Which case?"

"I don't know," Laura shrugged. "We always get the confession or the evidence required for an easy conviction. Say it's for one of the most wanted, or something."

“Then we’d have to hand the information over,” Nate said with exasperation. “You know what – I should follow my own advice from earlier and make sure that I’m the one telling the lie.”

“Well, do it quick,” Laura said. “We’re here.”

The looming shape of the building up ahead was so familiar to her that it felt like she was looking at something half-remembered from her childhood. She had that terrible prickly feeling of knowing she knew this place, but not really being able to grasp any memories that placed her there. She’d only seen it through the eyes of another – and that woman had been very familiar with the view. Laura knew that. She’d sensed that this was a route the victim often walked.

Not that familiarity had done anything for her in the vision Laura had seen.

She parked up outside Mickey’s, in a space right to one side. There was room for perhaps three cars – it was less of a parking lot and more of an incidental gap beside the building. Nate had just started talking on the phone, so she got out of the car to look closer and left him to finish up.

Mickey’s was out of commission, that much was clear. So much so that Laura wasn’t actually sure it would have still shown up on a map search, which was why it was so lucky they had Dean to rely on. The building was half-crumbling, bricks looking beaten down, paint peeling. Even the wooden boards placed over the windows looked like they were rotting away.

Which was strange, because Laura could have sworn in her vision that the windows weren’t boarded up at all. But maybe she was wrong. She’d seen it through the eyes of a panicked victim and in the dark, after all. And all the lights had been off.

She turned and looked the other way, towards the other side of the road. The trees crowded there just as she had remembered them. Unlike the rest of the street, the light of the day didn’t make them look less menacing. They were thickly entwined, some of the branches growing together, and Laura felt a lump in her throat at the thought of how desperate the woman in her vision had felt. How she’d sensed that going deeper into that terrifying mess of trees was the safest option.

Laura glanced over her shoulder and saw Nate getting out of the car, the phone back in his pocket instead of in his hand. “It was over there,” she called out. “On the other side.”

“Let’s go, then,” Nate said. He shrugged his FBI windbreaker closer around himself, folding his arms over his broad chest. “It’s cold out.”

“That’s February for you,” Laura said, eyes up to the sky. There were grayish-white clouds up there. She hoped it wasn’t an indication of snow.

There was no traffic on the road, so it was easy enough to cross. Laura led the way, looking back at Mickey’s until she knew they were about the right distance down the street, and then stepped off the sidewalk and into the darkness of the trees.

Immediately, the day seemed to almost disappear. The branches were so thick overhead that the only light coming in was from the sides, where the rays of the sun reached feebly down through the undergrowth. Laura picked her way carefully in a diagonal direction, trying to remember exactly where the woman had run.

“The man came from over there,” Laura said, turning to point behind herself. Nate looked, but there was nothing to be seen. Just more trees.

“Was he hiding?” Nate asked.

“I don’t know,” Laura said. “She stepped into the woods and he was just there. I don’t know if he was hiding in the trees watching the road, waiting for someone to go by, or if it was just a coincidence.”

“Why else would someone be in these trees?” Nate asked.

Laura shook her head. “I don’t know. I don’t remember it being this… dark. The light of the moon came down in a few places.”

“Were you seeing another season?” Nate suggested.

Laura shook her head again. “It’s winter already. If these trees were going to drop their leaves, they would have already. They must be evergreen.”

“Weird,” Nate said. He shrugged. “Where do we go next?”

“This way,” Laura said, leading him through the trees as best as she could. From time to time, she closed her eyes. The dream was still so vivid in her memory that she could see it if she shut out what was in front of her, almost overlaying it on reality. More than once, though, something confused her. A snapped-off branch that was whole in the vision or vice versa, a vine crawling up a tree trunk that she didn’t recognize, or a bush that seemed out of place.

But, finally, her feet led her correctly. They emerged out into the open space of the clearing – and there, ahead of them, was the cabin.

Laura frowned.

This wasn't right.

"This is it?" Nate asked, pausing in response to her hesitation.

"I…" Laura bit her lip, trying to think. "I'm sure this is it. But it looks… wrong."

"Wrong how?" Nate asked.

"Older," Laura said, which was the only thing she could really think of. "The place is falling apart."

"Okay," Nate said. "Well… could it be that the person who you saw – the male attacker – was living here? What if he moves in and fixes it up a bit? If we're here way too early, that would explain why everything looks a little different."

"Maybe," Laura said. "I guess that would explain why he was in the woods in the first place."

"Let's check this place out and see if anyone's living here right now," Nate said. "The vision – did you get the feeling this was his first attack?"

Laura considered it, measuring it against everything she knew about killers. "No, I don't think so. He saw her and he went after her right away. It was like he knew what he wanted and how to do it. This would be a serial offender. Even if it was his first kill, I would expect him to have assaulted women in the past."

"Then we might just have cause to bring him in if he's here already," Nate reasoned. "Let's find out."

Laura nodded and followed his lead as they walked up to the hut. The closer she saw it, the more confused she felt. It looked like the wood was rotting – just like it was at Mickey's. Part of the door had even been ripped off close to the top. But she was sure it looked like the door she had seen in her vision. Was it possible that someone had deliberately restored it to the way it used to look?

Or… was there something else going on here entirely?

"Hey!" Nate, who was in front of Laura and blocking her view, shouted so suddenly that she actually jumped. Before she had time to react to that, a dark shape darted through the opening door of the hut and flew to the side, and Laura found her body moving after it by instinct. It was only after she'd started to run that her brain processed the shape had to be a human – and therefore, maybe, the man she had seen in her vision.

There was nothing for her to touch to set off another vision, no way to predict where the man was going to run. All she could do was throw herself after him as rapidly as she could – with Nate at her side, shouting for him to stop, doing his best to outpace her.

The figure quickly darted among the trees, and for a moment Laura thought that was going to be the end of it – that there would be no way they would catch up with him. He would disappear into the thick branches and out of sight, with no way for them to figure out where he had gone without stopping to listen – which would only give him even more of an advantage.

Until the runner looked back over his shoulder to check how far behind they were –

And ran flat into a tree trunk, knocking himself to the ground so hard that even Laura winced.

CHAPTER FOUR

He sat back in his chair, reclining as far as it would go, and closed his eyes. These lunch breaks were sacred to him. He always came to a far part of the yard, a secluded place where no one would come to interrupt him. He turned his phone to silent. He blocked out any and all noise coming from the shop.

And then he was back there, reliving it, like it was a dream. More than a dream. Like he was back there himself.

It was a special pleasure for him to remember every single detail. He would start with the moment he first saw them, how he decided that they would be the one. How he watched them walk through the night, tottering helplessly like newborn foals on their heels, so clearly in need of someone to steer and help them.

Oh, how he would watch them. There always seemed to be some jeopardy at this point: Would they stumble and fall and injure themselves before he could even reach them? Would they break an ankle and howl into the night sky for help, or would they fall into the path of the one oncoming car that happened to pass at an inopportune moment?

As much as he wanted to take them himself, sometimes he would wish for that to happen. Sometimes he would linger in the pleasure of the fantasy, imagining them screaming and hurt and him not even touching them. As if he had made it happen with the power of his mind alone.

Ah, but it never had happened that way, not yet. So he would continue to remember, wrapping himself in the memory like a favorite blanket: how he had appeared to them and made their hearts race, flushed them with fear, the adrenaline surging in their veins. How they had begun to walk faster, even to run from him. Then the chase was on, the hunt, and he had pursued them, letting them think they were getting away. Letting them think that they had a chance.

Of course, he had already decided where he would pounce. He had chosen it all ahead of time, like picking out the menu for a five-course meal. And he took them when they came to the right spot, just like he was plucking rich and delicious berries right off the vine.

And then he devoured them whole.

His fingers twitched at the memory and he stirred, opening his eyes to look around and check he had not been observed. He opened the paper bag containing his sandwich and took it out, starting to eat it now that his recollection for the day was done.

It was always like this. At first, the memory was so fresh and so strong that he would feast off it for weeks and weeks, even months. But gradually, it would start to lose a little of its shine. He would shelve it alongside the others and bring them back into rotation, going over his favorites time and again. But then the years would pass, numbering in the multiple instead of the single. And he would start to feel like there was nothing new in those memories. Nothing worth re-living.

He would start to feel like he needed to make new memories. To scratch that itch that he felt deep inside, that urge that would not allow him to rest. He would start to feel like his lunch break was too long. That he needed something to fill it.

And then he would start to make a plan.

He was trying to be good, but things were harder and harder these days. He wanted to be good. He wanted to keep his hands clean. But there were all these little things, tiny things, that built up over time, like a wall made of matchsticks. And when they built up high enough, he had no choice but to knock it all down the only way he knew how.

To set it all on fire, and watch someone's life burn out of their eyes.

He shifted in his seat as he took another bite, thinking. Tonight, he could go out again and take a look at the route he had chosen. There was a lot to be practiced, tested, tried. He needed to make sure that his hiding places contained enough shadow. You couldn't simply turn up and hope for the best. You didn't want to be startled by a motion-sensor light coming on if you stepped back further from the road than you had before. You had to test things properly. You had to know if there was a security guard or if there was a hangout where local youths would break in to share beers on weekends. You couldn't just leave it to chance.

"Hey!"

A shout broke his concentration. He looked around, leaning his head out of the side window, wondering balefully who dared to disturb his lunch break. He caught sight of the young guy, the new one. He clearly hadn't learned yet. He didn't know that lunch breaks were sacred. He was too young and eager, willing to give up his own time even when they wouldn't get paid more for it.

"Boss wants us back at it," the kid called over when he knew that they had made eye contact. "He says there's a big job coming in and we need to be all hands on deck or we're not going to finish it by the end of the day."

He scowled, unhappy at the interruption and the disruption of his routine. He looked at the sandwich in his hand. This wasn't right. He was trying to be good, and things like this happened. Stealing his time. Taking his only rest and pleasure.

Well, only one way to make up for this kind of dissatisfaction. He would just have to make sure his lunch breaks counted for a lot more in the future by coming up with a new, fresh memory to treasure.

He shoved the rest of the sandwich into his mouth in one bite and got out of the half-wrecked car, trudging back towards the workshop with only darkness left in his mind.

CHAPTER FIVE

Laura caught her breath sitting on the step next to the man who had run from them, glancing around surreptitiously in the hope that the whole thing wasn't going to collapse in a shower of rotten wood and beetles. Nate stood guard in front of them with his arms crossed over his chest, enough of a menacing presence to seriously dissuade their fugitive from trying to go on the run again.

He was more of a boy than a man, now that he had his hood pulled down from over his ears. That, too, was disappointing. Laura had only seen the face of the attacker for a flash or two in her vision, but she knew he wasn't a kid. He was a fully-grown adult. So, unless her vision took place ten years in the future, this wasn't the man they were looking for.

"It wasn't occupied," the boy muttered crossly. "I didn't think anyone would mind. I swear. I'll just go."

"We're not here because you're living in the hut," Laura said, trying her best to be patient. "Although, you shouldn't. It's not safe. The whole thing looks like it could give way at any moment, and it can't be warm at night."

"Warmer than the side of the road," the boy muttered, still in that same surly tone. He crossed his arms over his chest defiantly, tucking his hands under his armpits as if to keep them warm.

Laura glanced to the side for a minute, looking at the trees and thinking. He wasn't their killer. But that didn't mean he couldn't be a witness.

"Have you seen anyone else hanging around here?" she asked. "Anyone who you thought was suspicious, any time of day or night?"

"No," he said. He shrugged. "Not many people come around here since the murder."

"The murder?" Laura asked, her heartrate flying through the roof suddenly.

"You don't know about it?" the kid asked, looking at her sideways and pointedly glancing at the FBI logo on her windbreaker. "I thought that was why you might be watching this place. Like, maybe you thought I was the guy who done it."

"No," Laura said, distantly, her mind running overtime. Why was he talking about something in the past? Was the case linked to the one she had seen, the one that hadn't yet happened? "No, that's not why we're here. But – do you know anything about this murder?"

"Only that there was a girl who got strangled," he said, lifting his chin and pointing it towards their right. The place where Laura had seen the attacker leap on the woman in her vision. "They found her over there. Some people say it's haunted or whatever but it's just an old hut. Not a lot of people come around here since then so I get to have some privacy."

Laura looked up at Nate, giving him a significant expression, her lips pulled tight in a grimace. He nodded back. This needed some further exploration.

"Why are you sleeping rough, kid?" Nate asked.

"None of your business," he said, wrapping his arms around himself tighter and hunching forward to physically avoid the question.

Nate moved his head to the side, indicating for Laura to go over and get back on the phone to figure out what was going on – they'd been working together for long enough that she could interpret that easily. As she stood up, he moved closer, taking her place.

"I can see about getting you a place in a hostel," he said, but the kid shook his head and spat to the side.

Laura wanted to see how the conversation played out and whether Nate could convince him to get some help, but she wanted to know what the hell was going on here even more. She took out her cell phone and quickly realized the signal was spotty. Walking backwards and forwards over the clearing, she found the one spot where she actually had enough signal to get anything.

Which was when the messages started coming through.

Just found a link to an old case with that location. Call me for the details.

It's an unsolved murder – call me!

Laura, why aren't you answering your phone? You've got half an hour and I'm calling your Chief!

Laura winced and quickly dialed Dean's number, putting the phone to her ear.

"Laura?" he exclaimed, clearly having been anxiously waiting for her to make contact. "Jesus! I was starting to think you'd been murdered for digging into this old case!"

"I'm sorry, there wasn't any signal here," Laura said. "I only just got your messages. What's going on?"

"I found a case linked to that old hut in the woods you were talking about," Dean said. There were a couple of mouse clicks in the background. "Listen to this: a young woman was found dead right next to the hut, strangled to death. She was just laying on the ground there – she'd been missing for a couple of days before they did a sweep through the woods and found her."

"What did she look like?" Laura asked, her heart pounding hard in her chest. A vision of… the past? Had this crime already happened?

"She was about five-six, Black, with I guess mid-length curly hair. She was wearing a thin black jacket over a sequined minidress when she was found. There were a couple of heeled shoes found in the woods as well, like she'd run and kicked them off."

"That's her," Laura said, closing her eyes momentarily. It all made sense now. The disrepair of the hut and Mickey's, the extra growth in the trees, this new kid living in the hut. It was the passage of time. "When did this happen?"

"Four years ago," Dean said. "Her name was Joy Kingsley. She was reported missing by her roommate. There wasn't enough forensic evidence to go forward with the case and they never found any suspects. The buildings there didn't have security cameras out front, so there's no information at all on what might have happened."

"Jesus," Laura muttered, holding a hand against her head. Joy Kingsley. No one had seen what had happened to her.

Except for Laura.

But what she was supposed to do with this information, four years after the fact, was something she had yet to figure out.

"Laura, how did you know about this?" Dean asked. "If you have footage of it happening, then you should hand it in to the lead investigator."

"No, it's not that," Laura said. "I don't have any kind of lead. I didn't even know that kind of thing happened here."

"Are you sure?" Dean didn't sound convinced at all. "Why did you need to know what she looked like?"

"Because…" Laura closed her eyes for another moment, wishing that she had put Nate on the phone instead so he could tell one of his so-called more convincing lies. "There was someone in the video, but she wasn't the victim. And she doesn't appear to come to any harm. I think it's just kids playing a prank, you know? Thinking it's funny to send in a video reenacting something that already happened to make us panic."

"Are you sure?" Dean asked. "The way you described it sounded a lot more sophisticated than just kids, if they have the ability to make it disappear like that."

"Isn't it usually kids that make the most damage hacking into government systems and stuff like that?" Laura pointed out. "Look, it's fine, Dean. I wouldn't mind getting the file sent over since we're here in the neighborhood anyway and we can take a look, but we don't need to do anything else about the video. Thanks for your help, anyway."

"Alright," Dean said, still sounding unsure. "Well, I'm always here if you need me."

"Thanks," Laura said again, before hanging up.

She turned to look at Nate, but he was still deep in conversation with the kid – who had now turned towards him with more open body language, like he was actually ready to listen. Laura didn't want to interrupt that. She walked back into the woods instead, retracing the way that she had seen Joy come.

Joy Kingsley, dead four years ago. Why the hell was Laura getting a vision now?

It had been so vivid and strong – more so than anything she had ever seen before. She just didn't understand it. She'd felt that her powers had been getting stronger ever since she'd been in contact with Zach, and then stopped being in contact with him so that the block between them could dissipate. She had known that they had come back not just as good as they were before, but even stronger.

But this…

This reminded her of when the block had been in place and everything had been so much more difficult to understand. Then her visions had been foggy and unclear, and they had also started to act up: showing her the past as well as the future. She'd thought they were fixed now, but apparently this seeing the past thing was here to stay.

If only she had a way to actually tell the difference between past and future visions, that would have been extremely useful.

“Laura?” Nate called out from the clearing.

“I’m here,” Laura called back, walking back towards him. When she emerged from the trees she found him standing, the kid by his side.

“We’re going to drop this one off at a shelter on the way out of town,” he said. “I made a couple of calls.”

“No problem,” Laura said, smiling at the kid but feeling like she was operating on autopilot while her mind went haywire.

“Oh,” Nate said, looking down at his phone.

“What?” Laura demanded, rushing closer in concern.

“Dean Marsters wants to know why you’re acting weird about this case,” he said, lifting it up to show Laura his screen.

Laura swore.

“One thing at a time,” Nate said. “Come on, you. Let’s get you to this shelter so you can settle in and get some lunch. Hot food sounds good, am I right?”

“Right,” the kid said, sounding a little grumpy and doubtful still. “For five minutes. And then I’ll be out here again.”

“I told you, didn’t I?” Nate said. “I put in a word for you. You’re getting the best, kid. Your own room in a fancy shelter and your own social worker to help you get back on your feet. You can even take my number so if they let you down after all, you can call and yell obscenities down the phone at me. And then I’ll help you again because it would be my fault it didn’t work out.”

“Okay,” he said, shrugging his shoulders like he was only grudgingly accepting. But Laura detected, underneath it all, that he was secretly pretty relieved.

***

“Okay,” Laura said, as soon as they were back on the road again. “What the hell am I going to do about Dean now?”

“Leave it to me,” Nate said. “I’ll talk to him when we’re back home. Are we going to the office, or pretending to stay out for the whole day?”

“We can’t wait until then,” Laura said. She felt a state of panic taking over her. In her mind’s eye, the consequences were clear. Dean would tell Division Chief Rondelle that there was something weird about Laura’s insistence on dismissing what seemed to be new evidence in a cold case. Rondelle would call them into his office and ask them to explain what had happened. Laura wouldn't be able to produce a video or any proof that there had ever been one – mostly because there hadn't been.

One way or another, finally, she would be forced to admit her deepest secret to her boss. The secret she had only told to two people: Nate, her loyal and trusted partner, and Chris – the man she loved. And now her boss would know about it.

And he would either think she was crazy and dismiss her from the FBI, or he would think she was dangerous and dismiss her from the FBI. Or, and she wasn't sure if this was worse, he might also believe her and make her spend the rest of her life in what amounted to indentured servitude spending every waking minute trying to force a vision in every single case going.

Either way, her life was going to move rapidly downhill from here – she could sense it.

Unless, of course, they stopped Dean from talking to Rondelle.

"What do you want me to do? Pull over and send him a text?" Nate asked.

"Yes!" Laura exclaimed. "Thank you. Look, I think there's a truck stop not far from here."

Nate rolled his eyes, but in a good-natured way. He pulled off at the truck stop and parked in the parking lot, taking out his cell phone and looking down at it for a long minute.

"What are you doing?" Laura asked finally in exasperation.

"I'm thinking of a good enough lie that he'll believe," Nate said, waving a hand towards her as though she was an annoying gnat. "Just give me a minute."

Laura slumped against the back of the seat with her eyes closed. She could see it all happening. Being called into Rondelle's office. Nate, of course, would vouch for her ability. Whether that meant Rondelle would believe her, or simply throw him out as well, Laura had no idea.

"Okay, done," Nate said, starting up the car's engine again.

"Wait, what?" Laura asked, her eyes snapping open. "What did you tell him?"

Nate smirked. "It's better if you don't know," he said.

"Seriously?"

"Seriously," he said. He chuckled.

Laura did not like the way he had chuckled. And the fact he'd had to make up a lie to fit the situation after it had already taken place didn't sit well with her, especially if she didn't know how well he'd managed it. She mentally braced herself to have to come up with something even better later – and God forbid that Dean mention the lie Nate had told before she was aware of it.

She felt her own phone buzz in her hand and looked down at it, expecting to see some kind of message from Dean that she would have to interpret to avoid contradicting whatever Nate had told him. Instead, it was Chris's name flashing up on the screen that had her heart stuttering a beat.

Are you at home today? I was thinking of dropping by.

Laura grinned, knowing full well she probably looked like an idiot and not caring, and fired off a response about being back in an hour or so.

"Hey, step on it, will you?" she asked, checking the time on the GPS.

"Why?" Nate asked, then glanced at her face. "Oh. You have a hot date to get back for. So, I guess we're not going back to the office."

"Probably for the best anyway," Laura said with a grimace, the specter of the daymare she'd had of Rondelle still looming large in her imagination.

Now all she wanted to do was get back home and see Chris – because she finally had another person she could speak to about what she could do. And because, ever since he had accepted her abilities and embraced her for who she was in full, she looked forward to seeing him more than anyone else. Except, of course, for her daughter – but Lacey was only allowed to visit Laura on her designated weekends.

"Fine," Nate said. "But tomorrow, we sit down and take a serious look at this cold case – and whether there's any way we can use your vision to solve it without alerting anyone about where we got the lead. And figure out why you're getting cold case visions now – because from what I've seen so far, your visions only warn us about present danger."

He was right, of course. Even when Laura had seen things from the past before, they had helped her to learn the identity of killers that were striking in the present time.

So the question remained, and needed to be answered: Why now? And what was the danger she needed to be aware of?

CHAPTER SIX

At the sound of a knock on her door, Laura shot to her feet and rushed over to it. Only at the last minute did she remember to take a breath, smooth down her hair, and actually smile – so she didn't completely terrify Chris and Amy with how eager she was to see them.

"Hey!" Chris said, beaming at her when she opened the door. Amy rushed forward and hugged Laura around the legs without a word, then rushed inside – perhaps looking for her playmate.

"Hi," Laura said, stepping forward lightly to kiss Chris and then aside so that he could come in. She glanced behind her at where the blonde-haired little girl was standing in the middle of the sparse living room, looking confused. "No Lacey here today, Ames. Sorry. She's with her Daddy today."

Amy's shoulders slumped a little. "That's okay," she said, unconvincingly.

"Someone had something they wanted to show you," Chris said, in an over-loud singsong voice, clearly directed at Amy rather than its ostensible target of Laura.

"Right!" Amy exclaimed. She spun around, taking off her tiny pink backpack, and rummaged inside it before bringing out a piece of paper – which got crumpled on the way out. She ran back to Laura excitedly and thrust it towards her.

"What's this?" Laura asked, taking the paper and glancing at Chris. He was smiling.

"Amy had to draw her family in class," he said. He sounded… Laura couldn't quite put her finger on it, but maybe it was something close to pride.

She looked at the paper, the drawing, and felt her heart nearly burst in her chest. The drawing was annotated, which was helpful, since Amy's artwork looked very similar to that of any six-year-old. But the four round, lumpy figures, each of which was drawn in a different colored crayon, did have names written above them – albeit names with backwards letters and misspellings.

Me, Unkul Chris, Lara, Lasy.

The translation was easy. When asked to draw her family, Amy hadn't just drawn her now-guardian, her Uncle Chris – but she'd included Laura and Lacey in the picture as well.

Laura suddenly found herself having to blink very hard to hold back tears.

"What do you think?" Chris asked. "Isn't it a good picture?"

"It's a great picture," Laura said. She met his eyes and had to look away again, but that only brought her eyes in line with the picture once more, and she turned and rushed to the fridge so that she could hang it up with magnets as an excuse to not have to look.

"Can I go play?" Amy asked.

"You want to play with Lacey's toys?" Laura asked, turning, and giving her a raised eyebrow – but a playful one.

Amy nodded sagely. "She wouldn't mind."

Laura bit her lip to hold back a smile this time. The thing was, Amy was right. Lacey loved Amy like a sister. They played together and shared toys every weekend. And even with kids she didn't love, Lacey had been raised to share. That was one of the good things Laura could say about her ex-husband's parenting.

"Okay," Laura said. "Go on into her bedroom and choose something to play with, then. But you've got to take good care of it so Lacey doesn't get upset."

"I will!" Amy declared, quickly disappearing now that she had secured permission.

"Well, I'm glad she's happy," Laura half-laughed. She turned to Chris, feeling strangely awkward for a moment. "Um. Coffee?"

"Very much so," Chris grinned, sitting down on her sofa. "I had a fully-booked morning, so when I got out to pick up Amy from kindergarten, you were the first person I thought of."

"Really?" Laura asked, grabbing two mugs from the cupboard. Her coffee machine was nowhere near as fancy as Chris's, but it would have to do. "Why's that?"

"Because when I'm tired and need someone to help me relax from all the stress, I know I can rely on you to do that," Chris said. When Laura looked back at him, his handsome face was relaxed into a smile that wrinkled the corners of his eyes. Was he trying to kill her today with a heart attack, or what? Because she felt like that particular organ had stopped, swelled, and almost burst at least five times since he came in.

“We had a morning of it, too,” she said, trying to smoothly carry on instead of falling into a puddle of goo in front of him. “We went into Maryland and back, chasing a lead that turned out to be nothing.”

“A lead?” Chris asked. “I thought you were between cases right now – isn’t that why you’re home?”

“Yeah.” Laura filled his cup and then her own, and walked them the short distance between the kitchen and the sofa. “It wasn’t a case so much as a vision.”

“Oh,” Chris said, nodding. He still wasn’t quite used to the fact that she had psychic visions. He accepted it, but he was still processing and understanding it. He was clearly trying to act normal in response to her news, but he was overdoing it, his head moving up and down far too vehemently.

Laura curled up next to him on the sofa with her cup, thinking that the best way to get him through this awkwardness was just to keep going until he was acclimatized. “I saw a woman being – you know, m-worded.”

“M-word…?” Chris followed her glance towards the open door which served as Lacey’s room, and his eyebrows lifted in understanding. While there was a risk that Amy could overhear, Laura didn’t want to say the gory details outright. “Ah. Go on.”

“Well, there’s not much more to the story,” Laura said, taking a sip. “We get there, and it turns out I was actually seeing something that happened four years ago. So, we were too late to save anyone, and I didn’t get any information in the vision that would help close the case, so I guess I wasted our time.”

“You saw the past?” Chris frowned. “Aren’t you supposed to see the future?”

Laura shrugged her shoulders. “Don’t ask me. I barely understand how this thing works, you know.”

“You’ve had thirty…” Chris left the end of the number dangling, but instead of filling it in, he caught Laura’s severe look and cleared his throat. “Thirty years to get used to this thing. And you still don’t get it fully. How long is it going to take me to get used to it?”

“You’ll get there,” Laura said. “Nate did. I called him at three in the morning to investigate a case I saw in a dream and he didn’t even bat an eyelid.”

“Hm,” Chris hummed.

“What?”

"Oh, nothing."

Laura looked at him. "You're jealous."

"No," Chris said, taking a sip of his coffee.

"You are!" Laura chuckled. "Oh, my God. You're jealous of Nate."

"Well!" Chris said, exasperated. "He gets to spend a lot more time with you than I do."

"I could say the same for you and your secretary," Laura said, getting huge enjoyment out of teasing him. "You see her all day long."

"Ah, not all day, and not every day," Chris said, holding up a finger. "Sometimes, like today, I only work a half day."

"It's not my fault you're a part-timer," Laura grinned.

Chris shook his head and rolled his eyes – though Laura sensed it was at himself, not at her. "Okay. So maybe it's a little ridiculous. But you did tell him first."

"Ah," Laura said. "But you're looking at it wrong."

"I am?"

"I told him after we'd worked together for four years," she said. "I've only known you for four months."

Chris tilted his head as if considering. "Actually, that does make me feel better."

"Good." Laura sipped at her coffee and Chris did the same, the pair of them sharing a more comfortable silence now. "I wish I could have done more, but I guess it's just one of those cases."

"Don't feel bad." Chris looked at his hands as he spoke, as if he was remembering something in particular. "Sometimes you just can't help everyone. I still get those patients that I can't save, no matter how hard I try. It's not your fault, same as it's not my fault."

"You're right." Laura reached over and touched his hand to reassure him – then instantly pulled back. What was that?

"What?" Chris asked, a worried look coming over his face.

"I'm… I'm not sure," Laura said. She took a breath, told herself to be brave, and reached out again.

The feeling that came over her was like being submerged in fog. Gray, light fog swathing around her, clouding the room and swallowing everything up. It was a similar experience to the aura of death she had, minor handful of times, encountered, but that was a clinging, cloying blackness. This was much lighter – but she had no doubt that it was just as serious.

"I think you're in danger," she said.

"From what?" Chris asked immediately, his eyes going wide.

Laura shook her head, unable to give him an answer. She was trying to think, to concentrate. She gripped his wrist harder, closing her eyes to focus, willing a vision to come. This wasn't like the awful, sick feeling she got from the aura of death – she could power through it. But nothing came.

"I just don't know," she said, helplessly shrugging as she let go. "It's not becoming clearer or giving me any further signs. I just have this vague, foggy feeling."

"That's reassuring," Chris said.

"Sorry," Laura replied, pressing her hands against her own forehead. "Sorry. I probably shouldn't have said anything. What a useless thing – to warn you against something without actually being able to say what it is."

"No, I guess it's good," Chris said. Laura got the sense that he was trying hard to take it well, for her sake. Under the surface of his words she sensed a current of tension, of fear. "I can watch out for things. I don't know what I'm watching out for, but I can be sensible. Like, maybe I won't drive too fast on the way to work tomorrow, even if I'm running late."

"Yeah," Laura nodded. "I would appreciate you being a little more careful for a bit. Until I get more details – or it goes away."

"Don't you have to keep touching me in order to make these visions show up?" Chris asked.

"I do," Laura smiled.

"I think I like the sound of this vague danger after all," Chris grinned. She had the impression that he was latching onto a joke in order to hide the very real unease he felt. Unease that centered around her – something she wasn't too pleased about.

Even though she smiled back, Laura couldn't shake that sense of unease. That something was coming. Something she didn't know, couldn't name. It wasn't the aura of death – but that didn't mean it wouldn't turn into one. And besides, there were plenty of things that were worse than death. Things that would make you wish that death had come for you after all.

All she could do now was stay vigilant for whatever it was that was coming for Chris – because there was no way in hell she was letting it get to him.

CHAPTER SEVEN

July looked down at the car keys in her hand, thinking. If she just focused, she would be able to get them in the lock. She just had to manage to control the swaying for a moment, and it would work. Left… no, right…

July stopped, the key clunking against the side of the lock yet again and not quite getting in. She couldn't unlock the damn car.

Somewhere in the distant recesses of her alcohol-soaked mind, she recognized that if she wasn't able to unlock the car, she probably wasn't in a fit state to drive.

July sighed, using both hands to push her hair back from her face and managing to tangle her keychain in it in the process. She yanked it free with some effort and felt a wince of pain that did a little bit of work towards sobering her up – though not enough that she could believe for a moment it was safe for her to drive.

She sighed, turned, and started walking.

It was only a forty-minute walk home, so that was good, at least. By the time she got back she would probably have burned off enough of the alcohol that she wouldn't be sick overnight. This had turned from one single drink with the girls into a night that was completely out of control, and July wasn't even sure how it had happened.

She glanced over her shoulder at the car with regret, then turned to carry on walking.

God, it was dark out. July stumbled a little as she walked, feeling annoyed at herself for choosing to wear heels. She couldn't walk in them without being in excruciating pain when she was sober, and when she was drunk, it was hard enough trying to stay upright on the earth as it rotated without adding heels into the mix. But she'd had to look pretty for a drink with the girls, hadn't she?

She took a deep breath of the clear night air, feeling how much fresher it was out here than closer to where she worked. There wasn't so much of the smog of everyday pollution out here. At night, in the winter with the air cool and the skies clear, it was actually kind of pleasant.

At least, it was definitely pleasant while she had enough alcohol in her to stop the cold from getting into her bones. July hadn't even zipped up her jacket yet – mostly, if she was being honest, because she wasn't confident she had the hand-eye coordination to do it.

She shoved her hands into the pockets instead, walking almost blindly as she concentrated on speed rather than accuracy, so glad that she knew the way home well enough to not have to do something like read a map or follow directions.

There was only one stretch of the journey that she wasn't sure about. Most of it took her through a built-up area, past homes and stores, most of which would still be open to cater to the late-night crowd. But to get there, first, she had to walk by a long stretch of road – maybe ten minutes in total – through an industrial estate. It was dark and full of shadows, and all of the lots were either vacant or occupied by companies that shut down at night, and every time she had to walk through here, it gave her the creeps.

It was probably a good job that she was walking through it while she was still totally drunk, instead of at the end of the walk, when she would be sober enough to be way more afraid than this.

At least, that was what July thought until she saw his eyes.

She was walking by the entrance to one of the factories, the gates hanging open, and she hadn't been aware at all that there was anyone nearby. Most of the traffic avoided this area – the bar had closed and the last patrons been thrown out at the same time as she was, and most of them had gotten in their cars and zoomed by already. A couple of taxis had gone by in the opposite direction, towards the bar, but neither of them had come back again. July had felt alone – confidently, comfortably alone – the kind of alone where you might sing to yourself or start dancing down the road because no one would ever see it.

Until she saw his eyes.

It was like he was a cat, his eyes catching the light from somewhere, maybe the moon, catching and throwing it back at her. She hadn't seen his body, all dressed in black. She hadn't noticed his face. But when he looked at her and blinked and that light flashed on and off for a split second, drawing her attention, she froze.

Just for a moment, she froze and looked at him.

And he stepped back into the darkness, and July forced her feet to start to go faster, stopping just short of a run.

She clutched her jacket around herself to stop it flapping as she walked, her heartbeat pounding in her ears suddenly loud enough to drown out anything else. She felt sick. She shouldn't have had so much to drink. She was going so fast she felt like she was going to fall over, and the only way to stop herself from falling over was to keep putting one foot in front of the other even faster than before, like she was turning a constant tripping motion into a run.

She glanced over her shoulder and saw him, sliding back into the shadows at the side of the road as soon as she was facing his way.

July didn't know who he was or what he was doing here, but she knew it was bad. She knew that she had to get away from him before she found out what he wanted. She knew that if there wasn't a car passing by soon, she was going to have no way to get ahead of him.

He was keeping pace with her, and she was in heels and still far more drunk than she wanted to be, and he was probably just biding his time to catch up.

July looked over her shoulder again and he was there – closer –

She gave a frightened whimper and turned to run, but even as she attempted to make her feet hit the floor for those first running steps, she found them tracing a path in the air instead, coming into contact with nothing. She was being carried, hauled, and then she hit the floor again but now she was looking at the inside of a parking lot, she thought, because the building was so dark it was hard to see –

She opened her mouth and started to scream, started to call out for help – only to have something clamp down on her mouth, something cold and slightly fuzzy like a glove.

"No screaming," he said in a half-whisper, his voice guttural and harsh, and July had never wanted to scream more badly in her life.

CHAPTER EIGHT

Laura woke with a gasp, the sheets tangled around her legs and her body soaked in sweat. She felt like she'd been the one running from a shadowy man, trying to keep her balance, but it had only been a dream.

No, not a dream. She knew what it was, now. It was a vision of the past – a past that had already happened. It was so clear, so visceral, like she was really there - almost like she was actually inside the victim's mind – just like the last one had been.

She was starting to see a pattern here. Strong, visceral, dream visions – they seemed to take her into the past. But the vaguer, shorter, less intense visions were the future. It made sense when she thought about it: it was easier to get a firm grasp on something that had already happened. When the future was still open, someone might think a hundred different things as the moment approached – but when it was past, everything was already done and set in stone.

That was how she saw it, anyway. If the visions changed entirely and pulled the rug from under her feet again, she wouldn't particularly be surprised. She wasn't going to hold her breath that she had actually figured something out about the rules of how this worked until she had a lot more data to judge by.

But, God, that vision… another woman, just like the last. Laura hadn't seen the man's face clearly yet again, but she could feel his signature the way any investigator would. A woman walking alone by herself in a secluded area – a place that had lots of shadowy hiding spots where it would be possible to commit a murder without being seen at all. A woman who was drunk, no less. Partially incapacitated, less able to run.

Laura found her mind running in overdrive already, trying to solve it. This killer took a lot of precautions. He was clearly not as confident in his abilities to take someone down as other killers she had seen; not only did he want time and privacy to do what he wanted, but he also wanted a victim who had severe disadvantages. Someone who wouldn't even be able to fight him off when the time came.

He seemed to thrive on fear, too. Both times, he had let the women see him. Both times, he'd had no qualms about just striking when it was easy – he seemed to want a little bit of a chase. He could have reached out and grabbed the woman in that last vision the first moment she saw him, but instead, he chose to follow her, chase her, take her down when she was terrified.

That got Laura thinking.

Was there someone out there who had managed to get away from him?

Was there someone out there who could give a witness statement that would help them to track him down?

Laura hadn't seen any clear or distinct clues about the place she was in, but she was willing to bet it would be somewhere in Maryland. Probably not very far away from the place she and Nate had driven to yesterday, which gave her more of a starting point.

She stayed in bed, laying down as if she actually believed she was going to be able to get back to sleep after a dream like that. There was no urgency, this time, and her head was still pounding. She needed to lay down, to recover from the lack of sleep she had yesterday.

What she had seen had happened in the past, and there was no one to save. The woman she had seen was dead. Laura knew that had to be the case.

But still it burrowed away beneath her skin, niggling at her, trying to make her get up so that she could investigate it…

Laura closed her eyes with determination, promising herself that even if she didn't manage to fall asleep, she would stay here in bed until dawn if that was what it took.

***

Laura sipped her third coffee of the day, looking up at Nate as he crossed the bullpen to sit down at his desk.

"Hey," he said, then frowned. "You look like you've been here a while."

"Since about dawn," Laura shrugged, draining the last of the cup.

Nate dropped into his chair and then wheeled it over to her, lowering his voice. Agent Fred Jones, who usually sat behind them, was out on a case somewhere – he'd been out all week – so they were more or less alone in their quiet corner of the office. "You had another one, didn't you?"

Laura nodded. She cast her eyes around the rest of the room just in case, confirming for herself that everyone else was too busy to pay attention, and then showed Nate the notes she had been working on.

"At first, I wasn't going to do anything about it," she said. "It was the same killer. The same MO – a drunk woman walking home at night past an area with a lot of shadows, where he was able to drag her out of sight. I knew it must have already happened and there was no point in trying to look into it to save someone – she's already dead. But I lay awake and I got to thinking."

"That's never a good sign," Nate said with a smirk.

Laura aimed a faux swipe at him. "Anyway," she continued. "I have to be seeing these for a reason. Right? I mean, okay – sometimes I see something really banal like someone dropping a cup of coffee, which I would never be able to stop without incriminating myself, and anyway, doesn't ruin anyone's life if it happens. But even when it's banal, I see it because I'll be there and able to stop it if I want to. I get shown things that I can personally have an impact on. I don't understand how any of this works, but I do really believe that."

"Right," Nate said. "So, your reasoning is that if you're seeing these cold cases now, there must be a reason. Like you think maybe you might be able to solve them?"

"Well, why not?" Laura asked. "We have more information than the original investigation did, by a mile."

"That's true, but we have to be very careful about where we source that information," Nate said. "As in, there has to actually be a source. Remember?"

"Right, I know," Laura said. "I'm just hoping that if we pretend I got interested in the cold cases out of sheer curiosity, we can bring something up via investigation that will actually help."

Nate shrugged. "Look, I'll make you a deal," he said. "You investigate the case, I'll keep going on our paperwork. It's got to be done by one of us. If this thing has legs like you think it does, then I agree that we should look into it, but we can't just drop everything else and then tell Rondelle we were just curious about the cases."

"Fine," Laura said. "But listen to what I've got so far. It's actually pretty compelling."

"Go ahead," Nate nodded.

"So, I used the location we were at last time as a starting point to search for the kind of place I saw," Laura said. "As it turns out, on the other side of the same town, there's an area of factories and warehouses. I used the street view and found the spot where I was in the vision."

"So, we're talking the same town?"

"Right. But this is the thing. The two cases – even though they were both cases of young women who disappeared on their way home from a bar and both were drunk, no one connected them at the time. Not even when the bodies were found and they both had marks of manual strangulation. There were two years between them, they were on opposite sides of town, different residences, no connection between the women – and the fact that they were coming home from a bar, it seems like the local cops just assumed it was some sort of drunken tryst that went wrong or a crime of opportunity."

"But same place, same MO, and you must have a feel for the guy – same killer?"

"Yes," Laura nodded. "It's definitely the same killer. We're the first ones to make the connection, judging by these files."

"Then we definitely have something," Nate said. "Are there any other cases?"

"I'm not sure yet," Laura said. "I looked up strangled women and it turns out there's quite a lot. I need to go through the cases more carefully, bearing in mind it's also possible that the killer was actually caught or even convicted in another case, so it's going to take me a while. But…"

"What?" Nate asked, tilting his head. He obviously already had the feeling that she was about to ask for something he wasn't going to like.

Laura put on her best innocent smile and asked it anyway.

"I think they both came out of the same bar."

"How is that possible?" Nate asked. "You said they were found, and stalked, on the opposite sides of town."

"I know, but I went into the case file for the second victim," Laura said. "Her name was July Hall. She went on a night out with friends that seemed to have taken them from one place to another. They started out at this one bar – The Major Hart. That's the one that Joy Kingsley was leaving when she was attacked. And if July's friends weren't quiet about where they were going next, someone could easily have followed them."

"That's an interesting theory," Nate said. "And this J thing – Joy, July. You think there's something in that?"

"I don't know," Laura said. "Two could be coincidence. I'd like three for a pattern. But if it takes this killer two years to pull off every attack, maybe he is that precise. Maybe he finds girls who fit his extremely particular niche, then stalks them relentlessly until they put themselves at risk. And I thought, what kind of person would be able to watch young women get drunk, find out their names, observe their state when they leave a bar, and all without raising suspicion?"

"A bartender," Nate said, picking up on her line of thought immediately.

"A bartender," Laura repeated triumphantly. "And if he's killing a victim every two years or so, and no one has noticed the connection yet, then he could still be out there. Serving drinks. Acting innocent. Biding his time."

Nate sighed and rubbed his eyes. "You want to go out there and talk to the people who work at the bar."

"If we can solve two, maybe more, cold cases, and stop a killer who is still out there, then don't you?" Laura asked. "This is way more important than paperwork."

"You do realize that if we don't do all of our paperwork correctly, some of our old convictions aren't going to be processed properly and other killers could walk?" Nate protested. But Laura didn't pay him any attention. He knew as well as she did that the paperwork they were doing at the moment was mostly the dregs of the boring admin that got left at the very bottom of the inbox because it was pointless and unimportant. No convictions were going to be vacated because they hadn't turned in their personal mileage expense forms properly.

"Come on," Laura said. "We can take my car. It's not that long of a drive. On the way, you can help me come up with the excuse as to why I was looking into these two cases in the first place so we can explain to Rondelle how we managed to link them. With this two-year gap, I'm nervous. I don't want there to be another victim this year – this month – even this week, when we could have done something today to stop it."

Nate sighed. "Let me get my coat on, at least."

Laura grinned in victory. "I'll meet you downstairs in the parking garage."

CHAPTER NINE

Laura pulled the car into the parking lot, turning off the engine and sitting to appreciate the scene for a moment. There was a lot that this place could tell them. It had witnessed both of the victims leaving, and at least one woman had gone on to die elsewhere.

"We going in?" Nate asked.

"I just want to get a feel for the place first," Laura said, craning her head to look up at the building. It was a secluded enough area, a short drive out of the town. They had passed the same woods they'd traipsed through yesterday, then moved on further until the bar loomed up, the only thing at the end of a short track with its own parking lot.

The building was kind of squat, made of red brick, and the windows appeared grimy. Laura knew, though, that there could be a big difference between the disgusting, slimy reality of a place in the daytime and the glamor that came with the cover of darkness – and the addition of copious amounts of alcohol to further obscure the senses.

She shrugged off thoughts about alcohol, trying her hardest to see this as a crime scene and not as a bar where alcohol could, if one wished, be purchased – and opened the car door.

"I think we have to play this smart," she said in a low voice as they both walked towards the main entrance. "We need to act like we're just looking for witnesses. If they know we suspect the staff, we could lose the suspect before we've even locked onto them. They might warn one another."

"I'll follow your lead," Nate said, sketching a mock bow and then opening the door for her to step through. "It's your case."

Laura flashed him a look of gratitude as she walked into the bar, grimacing even more as she took it in. It had the look of a room in which every single surface would most likely be sticky. She made a mental note not to lean on anything.

"Oh, hi," someone called out, sounding a little flustered. "We're closed. We don't open until five."

Laura turned towards the source of the voice, discovering a muscular, tall man in a black tank top with long blonde hair tied up on top of his head, matching a perfectly-groomed blonde beard. She made an immediate mental note that someone of his build and stature would have no problem at all with grabbing and strangling a young, drunk woman to death. He looked to be in his early twenties, but if she was off by even a short time – or if he'd been going to bars when he was underage – then he could be a candidate for both murders. "Hi," she said, opening her badge to show him. "We're not customers."

"Oh, geez," he said, turning and putting down a barrel he had been carrying without much sweat. "Uh, you probably want to talk to my manager."

"I'd like to talk to any staff who are on the premises, actually," Laura said. "Would you get them and bring them out here?"

"Yeah, of course," he said. He hovered momentarily. "Would you like a drink?"

"We're on duty," Nate said. Laura sensed he had jumped in to remove temptation – but she was doing fine. This place reminded her more than anything about the one thing that was true of alcoholism: No matter how good a time you thought you were having, as soon as you sobered up, you pretty much always discovered that you were in some grimy dive bar where all the surfaces were sticky and you wished you were back at home.

"Right. Have a seat," he said, finally disappearing back into a backroom, out of sight.

Laura looked down at the tables and chairs around them, hesitating.

Nate threw himself down on a comfortable-looking sofa, made in a sleek modern style to match chairs on the opposite side of a low table. He didn't immediately recoil in horror or disgust, so Laura gingerly joined him. She didn't stick to the leather, so she figured someone must have been thorough and cleaned this area at some point in the morning.

"Hi," a second voice, a female one this time, said. A woman was coming out of the same place the blonde barman had recently disappeared into, and he was right behind her. "I understand you wanted to speak with me? I'm the manager."

"Are there any other staff here on site today?" Laura asked.

"No, I'm afraid not," the manager said, coming closer to shake both of their hands and then sitting down in one of the curved armchairs. "We have a cleaner who does early mornings, but she's already gone home."

"That's alright," Nate said. "If you could take a seat, too…?"

The blonde barman, obviously missing the invitation to tell them his name, nodded hastily and sat in the chair.

"We're doing a routine follow-up on a couple of cold cases that are linked to this bar," Laura said. "It happens every now and then when we review the files to try to keep the cases going. I wanted to ask you some questions about a couple of women who disappeared from here."

The barman and the manager exchanged wide-eyed, startled looks.

"Really?" the manager burst out. She had dark hair cut into a bob which wobbled slightly with her every movement. "I haven't heard about anything like that!"

"This was a while back," Laura said quickly. "Four years ago, and two years ago."

Both of their faces cleared up. "I've only been here for just under two years," the manager said.

"Six months for me," the blonde barman said.

"We have a pretty high staff turnover," the manager clarified. "It's quite often college kids or just people who desperately need a job and will take anything. Sooner or later, they get a better offer, even if it's just a bar closer into town so they don't have to travel so far every day."

"That's a shame," Laura said. "Is there anyone on staff right now who has been around for that long?"

The manager shook her head. "I'm afraid not."

Nate frowned. "You don't have to go and look at your records?"

"I'm the longest-serving member of staff right now," she said. "That's how I got the manager gig."

"Right." Laura sighed. This was turning into a bit of a headache. If there was a chance for these two to warn anyone that the FBI were coming to talk to them, then they would lose the element of surprise completely, just as she had been afraid earlier. "Then, can we look at your employee records and see who would have been working on the dates in question?"

"I don't see why not," the manager said. "I'll just go get them." She got up even as she was speaking and quickly disappeared back into the staff area, leaving Laura and Nate with the blonde barman.

There was a moment of awkward silence.

"So, you said women disappeared?" he said, picking at the rip in the knee of his gray-black jeans and looking concerned.

"Two," Nate replied. "Actually, they were found. Murdered. Both of them."

The blonde barman's eyebrows shot up. "Woah," he said. "That's, like. Awful."

"Very much so," Laura agreed. "You haven't heard of anyone being murdered around her in more recent times, have you?"

The barman shook his head. "I don't really watch the news," he said. "I work late night shifts, so."

"You're here during the day," Nate said.

"Yeah?" the barman asked.

"It's daytime right now," Nate repeated. "Do you work days, or nights?"

"Oh!" he said, pointing at Nate as if he finally got the question. "Yeah, both. That's why I don't watch the news."

Laura blinked. She wasn't sure whether he was deliberately trying to mislead them and get them to ignore him, or whether he was just dumb and her suspicious investigator mind was working overtime.

"Here we are!" the manager exclaimed, walking out into the bar with a laptop held aloft. "I logged in already so you can see the system. It looks like there was a lot of staff turnover back then, too."

Laura's heart sank a little. "So, no one who worked for a long time period, like you?"

"Well, yes." The manager sat down, showing them the screen, and clicking on one of the entries. "Just the one. This guy was a bartender here when both of the women went missing, I guess, because he worked here for three and a half years. He never made manager, though."

"Huh," Nate said. "I wonder why that was."

"Some people don't want the responsibility, I guess," the manager said. "I can give you his details. This address might not be up to date anymore, but we wouldn't have updated it if he moved, so it's the best I can do. His name was Jayson Shaw."

Nate looked at Laura, his eyebrows shooting up. She could almost read his mind, what he was thinking. *His name starts with a J. Just like July and Joy.*

"Jayson Shaw?" the blonde barman repeated thoughtfully.

All three of the other heads in the room swung around to look at him.

"Does that ring a bell?" Laura asked.

“Maybe.” The barman shrugged. “I don’t know. But I think I heard my sister talk about him. She’s a couple of years older than me and she used to come here with her friends. That’s why I started coming here. And then I saw the poster that they wanted bar staff, you know?”

“What did your sister say about him?” Laura asked, praying for patience.

“Um, I think she was telling her friends to stay away from him,” he said. “They were all sharing stories. I got kinda like protective big bro, you know? Only, I’m the little bro, but like, I wanted to be the big bro type. They said he was, like, not someone you could trust if you got drunk. That he tried to hit on the girls who were almost passed out and take them home.”

That was a pretty big allegation. If he was taking advantage of women…

Maybe he was also taking revenge on the ones who said no at first, by making sure no one else could have them either.

“Well, thank you for that,” Laura said. She took her notebook out of her pocket and scrawled down the address and phone number listed on the spreadsheet as she spoke. “If you do happen to run into anyone who was working here around that time, or even a regular customer who might remember it, give us a call.”

“We will, definitely,” the manager said, getting to her feet to walk them out. “If two of our customers have been victims, then we need to do something about it. I haven’t really been doing this all that long, and I never really got any training on this kind of thing. Could you tell me anything – I mean, anything that we can do to make our customers safer?”

Laura considered that for a moment. “Tell your staff to watch out for women leaving on their own, especially drunk ones,” she said. “Set up a good relationship with a local taxi service, get them to have a cab on standby at all times during the night in exchange for making sure those single women get in the cabs. Don’t let them walk home alone.”

“And watch out for spiked drinks, too,” Nate added. “Your staff are likely to be the only ones who are sober in the place, so you have to make sure that they look out for your customers who might not be paying as much attention.”

“We’re already doing most of that,” the manager said. “The taxis wait outside because they know they’ll get the business. Sometimes at the end of the night, though, there aren't enough for everyone. I think people sometimes walk home because of that. Or because of the cost."

"Then you might consider introducing a shuttle service back towards the center of town, since you're so far out," Laura suggested. "If you charge to take groups and parties to and from the bar, you might even find your attendance going up. Personally, though, I'd offer the ride back as a free service for anyone who willingly turns in their car keys instead of trying to drive home."

"Got it," the manager nodded. They had walked to the door already, and Laura blinked slightly at the contrast in the bright yet pale sunshine that awaited them. "I hope you catch whoever did this."

"So do we," Laura said, grimly.

And with all those Js lining up in a neat little row, she knew exactly where to start.

CHAPTER TEN

When they pulled up on a suburban street that had everything just short of the white picket fence, Laura found herself frowning and checking the GPS twice.

"This doesn't look right," she muttered. "Does it? A guy who was working as a bartender lived here?"

"No, it doesn't," Nate said. "So, if he was working while living in… what? His parents' house? Maybe he wasn't able to take women back home with him."

"Let's figure this out," Laura said, shaking her head. "I'm not even convinced this is where he lives, but we'll find out."

She got out of the car, glancing up and down the street as she did so. It was a calm day, the sky clear. The street was dotted with cars, many of them hybrids or people carriers, and at least one neighbor within sight was mowing their lawn in the front yard.

Killers could come from any walk of life, of course, but in her experience, they very often didn't come from places like this. And if they did – well, those were the ones that usually tended to be the most terrifying. The killers who maintained a lovely family life with a wife and children and were pillars of the local community were the ones who got away with it the longest and often committed the most vile crimes. BTK came to mind.

Nate went ahead and knocked at the door before Laura caught up with him, but they were both standing on the doorstep when it opened. A brunette woman with her hair up in a high ponytail and a baby, perhaps six or eight months old, balanced on her hip, looked up at them in confusion.

"Hello?" she asked.

"Hello," Laura said, smoothly, as if she wasn't at all phased by the appearance of this slice of family life when she was expecting to find an ex-barman. "We're looking for Jayson Shaw."

"Oh, Jayson's my husband," she said. Her hand went up to her neck automatically, touching a pendant hanging there in the shape of a heart. A gift from him, no doubt. Laura quickly memorized its appearance.

She hated that she had to think this way, but there was always a chance that she was looking at a trophy taken from the neck of one of his victims. "He's at work right now."

"He is? What does he do?" Nate asked quickly, as if he was just very curious.

"Oh, he manages an entertainment complex on the outskirts of the city," Mrs. Shaw said. That raised both of their eyebrows.

"We need to speak with him," Laura said. She took the chance, now, knowing it could end up in him fleeing – but needing to build enough trust with the wife to at least open the chance. She took out her badge and showed it. "It's regarding something that happened at a bar he used to work at – we're just looking to check his witness statement."

"Oh, well, I'm sure he'll be happy to help," Mrs. Shaw said. She pushed the door open wider with her hip, the baby's eyes following the motion silently. "If you want to come inside, I could video call him for you right now – we always speak on video at lunchtime, anyway."

"That would be fantastic," Laura nodded. This could be a good opportunity. If it was him and he was spooked, then he would be spooked as soon as he knew they were on the way. This way, at least they would be able to talk to him before he had the chance to disappear.

Mrs. Shaw led the way into a home that was pleasant, airy, and open with all the walls, furniture, and flooring in shades of white, cream, and beige. It was also just lightly on the side of chaotic – every few feet there was an abandoned pacifier, or a muslin cloth that had fallen to the floor, or a toddler's toy. Still, Laura, who had raised just one baby, with significantly more mess, was very impressed when they turned into an open-plan living space and saw a toddler of perhaps three years old sitting in the middle of the floor with a toy train set.

"I'll give him a call now," Mrs. Shaw said, tucking the baby into a bouncer seat and grabbing a tablet that was sitting on the end of a plush gray sofa. Laura and Nate found themselves sitting close together on that same seat and waiting as she quickly dialed, the screen clearing not long after to a shot of a clean-shaven, clean-cut man in a blue button-down shirt against a blue sky.

"Hey, babe," he said, not noticing Laura and Nate right away. "How're the boys?"

"They're good," Mrs. Shaw said. "Honey, I have someone here who wanted to speak with you. They said it's about something that happened at one of your bars a while back?"

Jayson Shaw refocused on them, frowning but nodding. "Sure. What's this about?"

"Hi, Mr. Shaw," Laura said. "We're reviewing the files for a couple of cold cases connected to The Major Hart."

Immediately, his expression darkened. "You're talking about those two girls."

Laura didn't want to give the game away by reacting, but if she could have, she would have turned to Nate and raised her eyebrows. "That's right. Can you tell us anything you know about them?"

"Just that I can't believe their killer still hasn't been found," he said. He shook his head. "Honestly, I told the original investigators everything I could think of. I didn't know much back then."

Laura had looked up his statement in the car, and she knew there wasn't much to it. "Are you sure you can't recall anything else?" she asked. "It could be someone who wasn't suspicious until later on, for example. Something you overheard. Or someone who stopped coming to the bar right around the time of the second murder."

"A lot of people stopped coming to the bar after the second murder," he said. "That wasn't great for business. I ended up leaving, too. I didn't want to see another one."

"Why did you stay working at the bar for so long?" Laura asked. "We've seen your employee record. You were there for three years."

"So?" he asked, giving her a blank look through the tablet's screen.

"So, when we spoke to the current staff earlier today, they told us there's always been a lot of staff turnover there. Staying for more than a year is usually enough to warrant a manager's position. Yet, you stayed on as only a bartender for the whole time you worked there."

"That was simple math," Shaw shrugged. "I was working two jobs for most of that time – I had a shift at night and a shift during the day, and I would sleep a few hours between them on each side. They wanted me to go up to being manager, that would have meant mandatory work during the day to prep the place for opening. But the promotion didn't come with enough of a pay raise to cover what I was earning in my second job."

"Why the hustle?" Nate asked.

"I wanted to train in a number of different areas at once, as quickly as I could," he said. "I had my sights on something bigger. Now, here I am. I could have spent all those years getting managerial experience in one area of hosting, but instead I worked at other venues during the day and ticked off a lot more boxes. That's how I got the job I have now. And I did it faster than anyone my age."

"Still, it's interesting," Laura said. "Out of all the staff hired at the bar, you're the only one who was there for the duration of the time that both the women were killed after leaving there."

"Well, the second girl, she was killed after going on from our place to another bar," Shaw pointed out.

"Still," Laura repeated, looking dead into his eyes.

His expression darkened. "Are you questioning me as a suspect?"

"Should we be?" Nate countered.

"I can't believe this," he said, with a half-laugh that had no humor in it, raising his eyes to the ceiling. "I really can't believe this. You know the initial investigators already spoke with me?"

"I have their notes, and I know they only spoke to you after Joy Kingsley went missing, never about July Hall," Laura replied calmly. "I also have witness statements which suggest you were known to go after drunk women and attempt to get them to come home with you. What can you tell us about that?"

"I… ha, wow. I can't believe this." He shook his head, wiping his hand over his forehead. "I can't believe you've got it so twisted. No, I didn't prey on vulnerable women while I was working as a barman."

"We have multiple witnesses who believe you did," Laura said. "So, which is it? Are you lying, or are they?" The 'multiple witnesses' was a bit thin – all they really had was hearsay that more than one person knew about it – but she could stretch the truth a little if it would prompt a confession.

"They are," he snapped. "Or they're confused. Because whoever they think they saw preying on women, it wasn't me. I took my job seriously. And besides, by the time I worked there, I'd already started dating my wife."

"You were dating with two jobs that only allowed you a few hours of downtime for sleep in-between?" Laura asked with a heavy dose of skepticism.

"It was tough, but we spent time together when I was working," he said. "Maybe that's what people think they saw. I wasn't trying to proposition a random woman drinking in the bar – I was talking to my girlfriend. And, yeah, after my shift finished, sometimes we would go and dance for a couple of songs before we left. I had more stamina then. I could get by on only a little sleep. We were young."

"Alright." Laura shook her head slightly, glancing down at the notes she had made in her notebook. She didn't need them, but she liked the impression it gave, that she had more evidence to go on than she did. "But I'm still curious. You worked there longer than anyone else. You were the only person around when both women went missing. And yet, you don't have any idea about who could be suspicious in this case?"

"No, I don't," Shaw repeated stubbornly. His tone had completely changed, his body language shifted, from when they had first jumped on the call. He was angry with them for questioning him, perhaps doubly so for the fact it was happening in front of his wife. "I don't even know why you're talking to me. You can't have read the investigation notes properly."

"We read them," Laura said evenly. "We're reviewing everything. It's important to check things over when cases go cold."

"Then you must have seen the fact that security footage proved I was in the bar, still working my shift, when the second woman's body was found," he said. "I was behind the bar for the whole time. From her leaving the bar, to going to that other place, to leaving with her friends, to getting killed and then getting found – I never left the place once. It was a busy night. We were popular back then. I barely had a chance to breathe, let alone go out and attack someone."

That, finally, gave Laura pause. If there was actual indisputable evidence of an alibi, then Shaw couldn't be a suspect. She knew that the tapes would be in evidence somewhere; she hadn't seen them herself. It would be an easy check.

There was a chance, always a chance, that he was just lying to buy himself more time.

But what he said… it was beginning to ring true. The police at the time had questioned him thoroughly. It was all on tape. If they had dropped him as a suspect, there was a reason for that. The existence of a proven alibi would be a very good one.

"Alright," Laura said. "Well, thank you for your time. We'll be back in touch if we do have any further questions." That was enough to cover herself a little. She would go to the local precinct, dig up the footage, and watch it – and then she would know for sure.

For now, she started to get up, nodding her thanks at Mrs. Shaw, figuring the couple would want a little time to discuss what had happened in what might have been left of his lunch break.

"Wait," Shaw said, pulling her attention back to the screen. He was watching them closely, even leaning forward, as though he was keen for them not to leave just yet. "Don't you want to know who *did* prey on drunk women at the bar?"

Laura exchanged a glance with Nate. She sat back down on the sofa.

"We're listening," she said.

CHAPTER ELEVEN

Laura raised her hands in a gesture of impatience. "We're waiting," she said.

Jayson Shaw sighed, looking to the side. "I don't want to get anyone in trouble," he said. "I've moved on from that time. Really. I don't want to get dragged back into it with a court case or something."

"We understand that," Laura said. "But this is a double murder investigation. I'm going to need you to tell us what you know." *After all,* she wanted to add but didn't. *You're the one who spoke up and said you had something to tell us. Don't play coy now.*

"It's a rumor, kind of," he said, then made a face. "I saw it happening. But the thing is, it's a busy, noisy bar. I couldn't hear conversations, you know?"

"I think you've given yourself enough coverage, now," Laura said evenly. "You can go ahead and just tell us."

"Well." Shaw took another deep breath. "It was the guy who owned the bar. He wasn't around every night, and he didn't work any shifts – he just hired people to run it for him. But he would come in to drink. I saw him talking to women a lot of times, women who were way too far gone. After he'd leave to go to the bathroom or smoke a cigarette or whatever, I would go up to the woman and try to encourage her to go home with her friends so she'd be safe. I'm sure that's why people thought I was being a creep. But I was trying to save them from him, that's all."

"That's very noble," Laura said. "How can we be sure you're telling the truth and not just twisting the story to make yourself sound better?"

"Because he did it to me," Mrs. Shaw said, finally speaking up.

Laura blinked. "Excuse me?"

"The first time we met, it was not long after Jayse had started working at the bar. This older man tried to hit on me and at first I thought it was gross, but he said he had this big mansion and a flashy car and he wanted to give me a gift. The kind of stuff that wouldn't work if you were sober, but if you're drunk, it sounds great." Mrs.

Shaw took a deep breath. "The next thing I know, this handsome barman comes up to me and tells me I look like I've had too many drinks and I should go home – and not with a strange man I don't know. I thought he was being obnoxious, but my girlfriends took me home anyway. The next night, after I sobered up, I went back to thank him – and that's when he said I could thank him properly by letting him take me out on a date. A sober one."

"And that was four or five months before the first one disappeared from the bar," Shaw pointed out. "Just in case you thought I was lying to you earlier. We really were dating the whole time during the disappearances."

"Alright," Laura said. She had to push aside the question of whether or not they were lying and take things at face value for the moment. It was the only way they were going to get through to an end of this conversation. She and Nate could check the facts that were on record later. "This owner – what was his name? Does he still own the place?"

"I figure he does, if it hasn't changed the name above the door," Shaw said. "His name was Hart. John Hart. That's why he called the bar that."

"Then, thank you for your time," Laura said. "But we'd really better go. We have a lot of other avenues to check out as we review the case."

"Can you see yourselves out?" Mrs. Shaw asked, clearly keen to stay on the phone with her husband. As if on cue, the baby wailed.

"Yes, of course," Laura said.

She exchanged a look with Nate as they reached the door. They didn't even need to talk about it. It was obvious what they had to do next.

John Hart had some accusations to answer, and he had better hope he had two very solid alibis.

***

Laura rubbed her hands over her face, feeling like this whole day had been some kind of cosmic joke. "I can't believe we're back here again," she said.

"Yeah, well, let's just hope that secretary was telling the truth," Nate said. "If it turns out John Hart isn't here, I'm liable to throw one of his chairs through one of his windows. I'm not chasing him to another location."

"I know, I know," Laura sighed. "Christ. Getting to his home and then his office and not having him be at either of them was bad enough. If he's not here, I think we have to consider that she's warning him to stay a step ahead of us so he can destroy evidence or something."

"Come on, let's go in," Nate said, getting out of the car.

Laura followed him, noting his determination etched in every line of his body, starting with his fierce walk towards the bar. The Major Hart was turning out to be a real hub in this case, in more ways than one. It was the kind of wild goose chase that could make a woman think she needed a drink.

But she didn't, of course.

Right?

The bar looked much the same inside as it had earlier. It was still early afternoon, not yet time for the place to start flooding with patrons. The manager was sitting in an armchair in the corner, not far from where they had spoken to her before, and she looked up in surprise to see them again.

"Oh!" she said, clearly speaking to the person sitting in front of her – a person with their back to the two agents. "Oh, these are the agents I was talking to you about. They must have some more questions, is that right?"

"Yes, that's right," Nate said, letting his voice carry. The manager approached them as they approached her, and they ended up meeting in the middle of the bar space. "We're looking to speak with the owner of the bar."

"That's lucky!" the manager exclaimed, turning around. "John's right here."

It's not luck, Laura thought, if you had to spend all your energy and time chasing around after someone, to finally find them.

"John Hart," Nate said, which actually *was* lucky, because Laura wasn't sure how controlled her voice would have been just then. "We would love to ask you some questions about the time of the two murders that happened around here. We're reviewing the cold case files and speaking with everyone involved again."

"There was only one murder around here," John grunted, getting up. "And I wasn't involved in either of them."

The first thought Laura had was that this wasn't the right man. He had a gut, spilling out over the top of his jeans and only just constrained in a gray button-down shirt, while the man in her visions had been of average build.

But then she checked herself. The last vision she had seen dated back to two years ago. If someone really let themselves go – if, say, they had an injury that left them laying on their back for months and they got into really bad eating habits – wasn't it possible for their physique to change so drastically in that amount of time? Besides, she hadn't seen his face – and she didn't want to rule someone out at this early stage of the investigation just on something that she wasn't even sure about.

"Maybe we can take a seat," Laura suggested, leading the way back over to where John had already been sitting without waiting for permission. She wanted to make sure that she and Nate controlled this interview, not the other way round. If they could get John on the back foot, maybe he would slip up.

And if she could work in the fact that his name *also* began with a J, just like the victims Joy and July and also just like Jayson Shaw, maybe he would crack.

"I'm sure you've already been brought up to speed by your very conscientious manager, here," Laura said, earning a beam from the woman herself, who was hovering nearby as if unsure whether she was still needed. "So, let's cut to the chase. What can you tell us about the night that July Hall went missing?"

"July?" John grunted. "That's the second one? I don't know anything. She didn't disappear from here; she was at another bar across town."

"We know that," Laura said evenly. She was taking him in as she spoke. He was in his fifties now, she guessed. Could it be that he had perhaps been more prolific when he was younger? Had he only been targeting drunk women, and only over a longer period of time, because he was less able now to pull off physical attacks? "She was here earlier in the night, though."

"So what? So are a lot of people," John grunted. "Look, I don't have time to go over a hundred questions that don't lead anywhere. This was all covered the first time I spoke with the police. I have other businesses to get to."

“That’s right,” Laura said, latching onto it. “Your secretary told us you have quite a few local businesses. You’re a big deal in this town, aren’t you, Mr. Hart?”

“I suppose you could say that,” he sniffed, pride puffing out his chest even as he acted like it was nothing.

“Then why do you keep hold of this place?” Laura asked, gesturing around. “It’s not exactly the most reputable venue in your repertoire, and with the two deaths, I was told it had a pretty bad reputation a couple of years ago.”

“That’s why I didn’t sell it,” he said, grunting in displeasure. “I couldn’t find anyone who wanted it. They were all telling me it was tainted. Well, I’m laughing now, because reputable or not, it pulls in the most profit of any of them on a Friday and Saturday night.”

“So, it’s purely a business decision?” Laura asked.

“What the hell else would it be?”

Laura noted his antagonistic response, the way his body language was open and wide and yet aggressive, as if he was trying to show that he was the most dominant person in the room. It was all adding up to something. But did it add up to the figure she had seen in her vision, who liked to quietly scare women instead of announcing his presence aloud?

“We had a report from a former employee of yours about some questionable behavior he observed during his time here,” Nate said. “Apparently, you were seen on multiple occasions trying to take advantage of women who were far too drunk to tell you no.”

“What?” John exploded, standing to his feet. He had that explosive kind of rage, the kind that manifested itself in shouts and displays of macho posturing, hitting the table and jumping to your feet. Laura could see that. She wasn’t sure it matched up with what she had seen. But that didn’t mean it wasn’t the same man – because whoever killed the women wasn’t necessarily enraged at the time that he did it. “How dare you come into my bar and say that to me?”

“I’m not the one saying it, Mr. Hart,” Nate said, handling the situation as calmly as he always did. “It’s a report that we received. We’re duty bound to check it out.”

“Well, you can cross that off your list and throw it away!” Hart shouted. “Taking advantage – I’ve never heard such bull! Girls like me. They know who I am. I’m a big deal around here. They want to go back to see my sports cars and my art collection. They want me to buy them Gucci. If anyone gets taken advantage of, it's me!"

Laura had no doubt in her mind, now, that the man was a creep. From what she had heard, from his severe reaction, she knew for a fact that he was taking advantage of women. She even knew that he knew what he was doing was wrong. He had to. That was the only reason why he would have that look on his face, that rage, that need to urgently dispel the accusations.

But did being a creep make him a killer?

Laura had an itching feeling up her spine. It told her that their suspect wasn't this type. That he didn't approach women in the open. If he could do that, if he could just have them eating out of his hand, then he wouldn't need to stalk and kill them. In fact, Laura was leaning more towards the idea that the killer was someone who was afraid to talk to women face to face, not a womanizer.

There was one way they could clear it up, and that was by sticking to the case itself – instead of wasting time going around the area with these suspicions and rumors.

"Where were you on the day that the first victim, Joy Kingsley, was taken from outside this bar?" she asked, meeting his gaze direct and unwavering.

"When that first one happened, I wasn't even here. I was on vacation," he said, sitting down in his seat again and slinging his arm across the back of the chair. "That should be in the notes in the first investigation."

"It isn't," Laura said. "In fact, you weren't even mentioned in the first investigation."

"See? Because they knew I had nothing to do with it. I wasn't even in the state," he said. "Look, I've got to get on with running my businesses. Time is money. So let's wrap this up."

Laura hated this man, even though she barely knew him. There was just a sense about some people, and she had the sense that John Hart was as sleazy and sticky as the bar he owned. But there was nothing she could do about that, not without proof and victims and people who actually wanted to press charges. There was nothing she could even do to keep him here, since he wasn't under arrest. He could leave whenever he wanted.

"Fine," she said, standing up so that at least she had the physical power for a moment. "But I would advise you not to leave town without speaking to the local precinct first. We may need to interview you again. And I'm going to need you to send over proof of that vacation – ticket receipts, travel stubs, anything that would prove you were where you say you were."

She wasn't even going to warn the local precinct. She didn't need to know when Hart wanted to leave town. But it might stop him from going out for a while, and when he did feel the need, he would get some pretty baffled looks. The thought was enough to appease the rage that was whirling in her stomach just a little.

Nate stood with her and lingered for just a moment, looking down at Hart, and Laura knew that he was playing out his own revenge in his own way, trying to intimidate him. There was a little comfort in the thought that maybe he wouldn't be so obvious with his behavior for a while if he thought that a big, burly FBI agent was watching him. Somehow, though, Laura doubted it. Men like that knew they could continue to get away with whatever they wanted.

She took a deep breath of the air outside as soon as she was out through the door, feeling like she needed to go somewhere to wash her hands and change her clothes.

"What now?" Nate asked in a low voice as they approached the car. "We're at a dead end. Pun not intended."

"Now, we do what we always do," Laura said. "We find the killer by looking at the victims. Come on. We'll find somewhere to sit and go through everything we know about both of them – and when we find that connection, we'll know who we're looking for."

Of course, she added to herself privately, that was only going to work if there really was a connection between the two victims.

But without that, they would have nothing to help them get any further on the case – and Laura didn't want to admit defeat yet. Because she was sure a man who had killed two women in such a way wouldn't have stopped there – and it had not escaped her notice that with two years between each of the cases, the next two-year period would land right about now.

CHAPTER TWELVE

Laura closed the door and looked around with a nod. "This will do very nicely."

Nate chuckled to himself. "I don't know how you think of these things."

"Well, I heard about private soundproof study rooms online," Laura said. "I had an idea the local college would have one, and here we are."

"In a student library," Nate said, with barely suppressed mirth. "Hey, are you sure they're totally soundproof?"

"I'm not certain you would get away with playing a drum kit in here, but we're just going to be talking at normal level," Laura said. "And you can't hear anything from out there, can you?"

"No," Nate admitted. He chuckled again. "The librarian's face when you showed her your badge and said you wanted to requisition a study room."

"Alright, alright," Laura said. "We need to focus here. Let's dig into them as much as we can."

"It might be difficult, you know," Nate said. "I know we would normally comb through social media profiles for some kind of a connection, but what I'm worried about is that anyone who died four years ago isn't going to have much of an online presence left."

"I know," Laura said. "But we still have to make sure we do all the possible checks we can before we move forward with this. If there's even the tiniest possibility of a connection between them, we need to know. I want some ammunition if we're going to go and speak to either of their families – I don't want to stir up that old grief if we don't actually have anything new to bring to the table."

"I get it," Nate said. "But don't you think the bar is connection enough? They might have met each other there, and we'd never be able to disprove it."

"Unless we can show that, for example, July Hall never went to the Major Hart before two years ago," Laura pointed out. "If their paths crossed in a bar, that's one thing. I want to find an actual connection. A mutual friend, an interest group, the same class at school – anything that we can actually use as a lead."

"I get it," Nate said, though there was a touch of weariness in his voice. "I'll start going through different sites. How do you want to divide them up?"

"Oh, we're not dividing them," Laura said. "You're working on connecting them. I'm going to investigate the bar."

Nate frowned. "How come you get the fun bit and I get the long, tedious, and probably ultimately unrewarding bit?"

"Because it's my case," Laura grinned. "Anyway, I've got to look at endless pictures of drunk, stupid people, so it's not all fun."

Nate's face dropped. "Will you be alright?"

Laura brushed him off, waving a hand. "I'll be fine."

She bent over the tablet she had rented along with the room, quickly searching for and loading up the bar's website, studiously avoiding his gaze until he looked away and got on with the task at hand.

She found a few galleries on the bar's site, but they only seemed to be illustrative of the facilities they held – there was no long-running gallery of all the people who'd been present on certain event nights, something that always used to come up in the past. Times had moved on, which was a shame – it had always been a good investigative tool, looking through months or even years of past event footage.

Laura navigated to their social media instead, looking through photo after photo, seeing all the images the bar had posted as well as the ones they had been tagged in. There were thousands – far too many to take them all in one sitting.

Luckily, she didn't need to take in all of them. In each case, she scrolled back as far as two years ago and then looked for posts made around the time that July Hall had died. She even found a few news posts in which the bar was tagged, talking about the case. She noted the comments on each one, scanning the usernames, trying to store them away in some compartment in her brain. It wasn't unheard of for killers to insert themselves into the online dialogue about their victims.

Even though she went back over the course of a whole year, though, she couldn't find any images that contained July Hall just enjoying the bar as a regular patron before anything happened to her. If she had been there before the night when she was killed, there was no evidence of that just yet.

Laura scrolled back further, but the bar had apparently not held an online presence four years ago – or if it had, all those old posts would have been archived or deleted. She sighed, shifting to the side to lean on one of her arms as she thought.

At the same time, Nate also shifted in his seat, and their arms brushed together.

Immediately, Laura felt it.

The same gray fog that had surrounded Chris was also all around Nate, hanging heavy around him like tendrils of mist, swathing him completely. Laura felt the room swim, feeling as though she'd driven her car right into the middle of a rolling bank of clouds.

She pulled her arm away, looking at Nate, and trying to actually see him, reading his face and body for any sign of anything that might be wrong with him.

"What's up?" Nate asked, feeling her intense scrutiny and taking on a worried expression himself.

"I don't know," Laura said. "Something's wrong."

"With the case?"

"With you." Laura swallowed. "I don't know what it is – it's new. I never felt it until this week, but the same thing happened with Chris. There's some kind of… some kind of aura."

"Like the aura of death again?" Nate asked, recoiling slightly. She had told him, of course, about the way she'd known she needed to save his life. The way she'd sensed death clinging to him months before it actually tried to strike.

"No," she said quickly. "No, it's not that. Something different. Danger, maybe?"

"I'm not sure danger is much better than death!" Nate objected, then paused. "No, actually, death was much worse. Are you seeing anything? Any clues to what I need to look out for?"

"No," Laura said, shaking her head. "It's like I'm stuck in fog. Everything's just vague and cloudy. I wish I knew what it meant, but it's brand new, and I don't know how to interpret it yet."

"So, I'm kind of like a guinea pig right now?" Nate asked. He made a face. "I don't know if I like this."

"Well, Chris is a guinea pig too, if that makes you feel any better," Laura said, snapping a bit more than she meant to. Did Nate think she enjoyed having to give out these vague warnings? She couldn't even tell the people she cared about what kind of danger was coming for them, or even if she was right about it being danger in the first place. She didn't want this.

"Not much," Nate said. "Though I guess if something terrible does happen, it sounds like it's going to happen to him first."

Laura stared at him.

Nate held up his hands in surrender. "Okay, I just tried to save myself with a very terrible joke and it didn't work. I'm sorry. I know you wish you could tell us both what to watch out for. I just feel a little… unsettled, I guess."

Laura sighed. "I guess I would, too, if someone told me I was in danger but couldn't actually give any concrete details."

"Are you?" Nate asked. "I mean, if Chris and I are in danger, doesn't it follow that you are too?"

Laura bit her lip. "I have no idea," she admitted. "And no idea how I would tell. I can't have visions about myself. At least, not auras, anyway."

"I guess that would be annoying," Nate said. "Seeing something in the corner of your vision all the time."

"It's not even the corner," Laura said. "It takes over everything. It's really like the room suddenly fills with fog."

"Do you think it's something to do with this case?" Nate asked. "Like, maybe we're looking into something we shouldn't?"

"No, I don't think so," Laura said. "I saw the aura around Chris before the second vision, so I had no reason to carry on investigating then."

"Alright, well, if you're sure," Nate said. "Look, I found a few people they have in common."

Laura wasn't sure about anything – and she'd managed to get wrapped up in the aura so much that she wasn't even sure what he was talking about for a moment. Then it clicked: their two victims. A few people the victims had in common.

"Are we thinking there's a connection with someone they both know?" Laura asked, feeling at least a flare of excitement that they might be about to find something.

"I don't know," Nate shrugged. "From what I've been able to find out, we're talking about a few casual acquaintances they had in common. It's not like one of them was best friends with the other's ex-boyfriend or something close like that. More like – if two people are going out in the nightlife in the same area, sooner or later there will be a bit of overlap in the people they know."

"Damn," Laura muttered. "Well, at least we have some vague leads to follow if nothing else comes up."

"Then what else do you want to look at? Did you find something with the bar?"

"No," Laura said. "Actually, there's no social media that dates back as far as when Joy Kingsley disappeared. And the more I think about it, the more suspicious that is."

"You think they tried to cover it all up and change their image?" Nate asked.

"I do," Laura confirmed. She took a breath. "And I think we need to look for more cases that match the victim profile and MO we have – because I don't think this killer has only struck twice."

CHAPTER THIRTEEN

Laura was sure her intuition wasn't going to let her down on this one. With access to the local precinct's system to conduct searches, all they had to was find the other cases that matched – because she knew the difference between a killer who knew what he was doing and one who was just starting out.

In her visions, he knew what he was doing. He had a pattern. He didn't hesitate. There was no fumbling, no letting the woman almost escape. He'd been waiting on purpose for them to come by – though how he might have known Joy would go into the woods, Laura didn't know. Perhaps that was just luck, and he'd been planning to lurk out of the trees at her.

But there was nothing of the nervousness or impulsiveness that would characterize a first-time crime. None of his actions were by accident. He knew where to wait to get them. He knew how to make them afraid, to let them run from him even though he was faster and stronger, and he knew when to take them down and kill them.

He'd done it before.

And, as the saying logically followed: he would do it again.

"Okay, here we go," Nate said. "We need to set our parameters."

"We should search for any women who disappeared from anywhere in town or even outside the town borders," Laura said. "Maybe set it to the last twenty years to start with. We can refine the search down after we know what we're dealing with."

Nate typed in what he'd been told, clicking on a few boxes and sliders, and then they both sat back a moment to let the results load.

When they did, Laura pressed her hand to her mouth.

"That's a lot of results," Nate said, vocalizing what she was also thinking.

"How can there be this many disappearances in one area and it not be flagged up?" Laura asked.

"I don't know," Nate replied. "But we need to narrow this down some. They're not all going to be relevant."

"Okay, let's look at removing the ones that have been resolved and found alive," Laura suggested. "Also, we can take out any that were killed by other methods. Any shootings, stabbings, anything like that – if they weren't strangled, we shouldn't consider them."

Nate nodded as she spoke, doing his best to refine the characteristics of the search as much as he could. When he was done and the list refreshed, it was significantly smaller.

But that was still worrying in itself. To see a list with more than a couple of names, when narrowing it down to just women who had disappeared without a trace or been strangled to death in a small area, immediately brought suspicion to mind. Something was off, here. Someone was killing girls.

"Let's look at the cases," Laura said, her mouth dry. "We're looking in particular for anyone who was last seen at a bar, or drinking with friends, before going off alone."

"There's Joy and July," Nate said grimly. "At least we know our search results are working if they both came up."

"What about the next one?"

Nate dutifully clicked on it. "Let's see… she went missing after hiking in the woods alone. This was twenty years ago, right at the limit of our search parameters. I guess search equipment and cell phone technology wasn't as good back then."

"Never found," Laura said. "I don't think we should include her as a potential. She was probably trapped or fell somewhere, starved to death, and got eaten by animals."

Nate made a face. "Geez."

"You know I'm right," Laura muttered. "Next one, come on. Let's get through these."

"Alright, next one… Abducted by her own uncle and found two weeks later," Nate said. "We can skip that one, too."

"Next one?" Laura asked, taking the opportunity to read this one as it came up. "Found in a wrecked car a day after being reported missing, down a ditch. Next."

"This one was drunk, but according to the witness reports, she likely slipped and fell into the river and then never came up," Nate said.

Laura sighed in frustration. "Are we seriously saying that this many women have been reported missing around here and it's all just coincidence?"

"Not yet, we're not," Nate said. "There are still a lot of names to go – oh, look at this one."

Laura read from the screen. "Reported missing after leaving downtown area bar… found strangled by roadside on outskirts of town in a quiet area. What's the date?"

Nate scrolled down. "Six years ago."

Laura hit the desk, causing the two local cops who were quietly working on the other side of the room to look up in alarm. She waved at them in a quick apology, then returned to the screen. "I knew it," she said. "This is him. This is a pattern. Once every two years."

"It's not exactly two years, though," Nate pointed out. "It's not the same date each time, or even the same month. They seem to be happening at random times through the year."

"That doesn't matter," Laura said. "It's once every couple of years. Something happens every couple of years – or maybe that's just the period he needs to cool down from the last one and start feeling that irresistible urge again."

"Then let's look back at eight years," Nate said, refining the search again.

Laura held her breath and bit her lip.

Then it came up: three results. Nate clicked on two of them and ruled them out quickly. "This one is a suicide… let's see the other… no, this one is domestic abuse. Looks like she ran away from her husband and he filed a report, but she was in a shelter in town the whole time."

"And the last one?" Laura asked, feeling like her heart was beating inside her throat.

Nate opened it and they both read in silence, looking for any red flag that would tell them it didn't fit the pattern.

"This fits," Nate said with some excitement. "A drunk woman, heading home on foot from a bar, found strangled to death in a quiet alleyway behind several disused buildings. He must have waited until she walked by there and then pulled her in."

"It fits perfectly," Laura said. "Two years ago, four years ago, six years ago, eight years ago. How far back does it go?"

"Only one way to find out," Nate said grimly. He clicked around on the screen, changing the parameters once again, keeping everything the same but the year. Ten years ago.

One result came up.

Nate clicked on it, and they both read with bated breath.

"A single woman walking home from a bar," Laura said, the words almost choking in her throat. "Taken and strangled in an area of woodland, but it looks like not the same place as before. Somewhere in the south of town. It was St Patrick's night. They must have been dealing with a lot of drunken incidents, and this one didn't get the amount of manpower it deserved."

"Twelve years ago?" Nate asked, searching one more time.

The system returned no results.

"Then that's it," Laura said. "Ten years he's been operating for. At least, ten years here. It's possible he might have targeted a different area previously."

"Or gone to three year intervals, instead of two," Nate said. "Maybe he sped up over time."

"Or his earlier victims weren't found, or weren't reported," Laura said. She rubbed her forehead with one hand. "We could sit here all week running different searches and checks, trying to ascertain whether St Patrick's was his first. We need a full team if we're going to do that. We can't do it alone, not when we're not even supposed to be here right now."

"But we have information now," Nate pointed out. "We know enough to put a profile together. We have five victims."

"July Hall, Joy Kingsley, Alayna Honeysett, Sarina Waterman, Allison Park," Laura said, reading their names in reverse chronological order. "So much for our idea about them being connected to the letter J."

"This is good," Nate said. "It means we're not wasting time chasing down something that doesn't actually have any bearing on the case. And we can see his MO clearly here. Each time he goes to a different bar, he picks a woman who seems to be random, and he waits for her to go through an abandoned or secluded area so he can kill her without being disturbed."

"It's only the fact that the last two victims were at the same bar at different points in the night that would even connect these cases at first glance," Laura said. She reached over and clicked the mouse on the printer icon, thinking they should have physical copies of these files to look over. "I'm not surprised no one connected them otherwise. They look like random attacks."

"And with the time between them, I'd bet there aren't a lot of officers here who are still working the same type of cases over the whole ten years," Nate pointed out. "People quit, retire, get promoted, move to different cities or different departments. Without one person working on every case and spotting both the MO and the time between each case, it would be almost impossible to put them together. Young women getting strangled on a night out – it's sad to say it, but it's not rare enough to raise huge eyebrows."

"Especially not when they have the volume of other cases," Laura agreed. "The other disappearances and, I'm sure, other murders of women. And given they weren't all even found the same night they disappeared, I'm guessing there was sometimes suspicion of other types of foul play – maybe a woman being abducted and kept for a few days was a possibility in some of them."

"Definitely for Allison Park," Nate said, pointing at the screen. "She wasn't found for three months. By then, they had no real way of narrowing down the date of her death precisely enough. They just knew she'd been dead for the majority of the time, but not whether it happened immediately or not."

"Well, I'm glad we've put this together," Laura said. "Maybe there's a way to connect them and get some justice, find a way to link together what little evidence there is. There's just one thing that bothers me."

"What's that?" Nate asked.

"Why now?" Laura gestured with her arms wide apart, as if to signify how random it all felt. "Why am I getting visions of something that happened two years ago, four years ago – right now? I normally see things related to something I'm close to. Something happening near to me. Why am I getting this vision of something that happened years ago and that wasn't even on our radar?"

"Maybe he's about to switch to men, and that's why I'm in danger," Nate joked. It fell flat, and even he realized it, making a grimace. "I don't know, Laura. Maybe we're just supposed to solve it. Maybe it's because you're the only person who can."

"Maybe," Laura sighed. As ever, she would have to put up with speculation instead of actually knowing the answer. It was always the same with her visions. So many questions, never enough answers.

"Well, let's -" Nate began, but Laura didn't find out what he was going to suggest. He cut himself off, looking down at the desk and his cell phone ringing on it, flashing up a name that made them both exchange a look of panic.

Chief Rondelle.

CHAPTER FOURTEEN

The psychic tapped aimlessly on the side of the steering wheel, glancing around without much understanding of where he was supposed to go. He knew he needed to be in D.C., but that was it. He needed to narrow it down somehow.

He'd seen an apartment building when he saw her, a few times now. He'd somehow hoped he would get here and just see it, just like that, recognize it from the road. It hadn't happened yet. He knew that she would be at the FBI Headquarters on a normal day, but that was too much of a risky place to stake out. Too many people who knew what they were doing would be looking out of the windows. He couldn't risk stalking her there.

A headache hit his temple like a ton of bricks and he gripped the steering wheel tightly for a moment, glad he had chosen to park, not knowing that this was coming –

She was wearing black, standing by the side of a grave.

"I can't believe it," she was saying to someone. The Black man – the one she was partnered up with for work. The big one that the psychic always considered to be the biggest threat in pulling all of this off. He was going to have to wait – to get her on her own. "I just can't believe he's gone."

"I know you searched for him for a long time," the big one said, his tone sympathetic.

"And then when we did find each other, we couldn't even stay together." Laura rested her hand on the gravestone. "It's so cruel. To have these powers, and to have to stay away from everyone else like you because of what it does to those powers."

The psychic, if he'd had a corporeal form in these visions, would have smiled. Oh, she didn't know. She didn't know why it was important for the powers to be diminished once two psychics came close to one another. She didn't know that killing one, consuming them, would allow you to absorb their power. She'd known another psychic – and she'd never taken advantage of it.

He would correct that mistake.

"Do you want to investigate?" the big one asked. "I know the locals said they were going to do everything they can to find out who killed him, but..."

"I do," Laura said. "I do want to. I know Rondelle will argue with us, saying it's not our kind of case, but I need to do right by Zach. He didn't deserve this."

Zach... the psychic realized he could read the name on the gràvestone. Zachary Kingston. The time between the two dates engraved on it was long. He had survived a long time, for one of his kind. What a shame that the psychic hadn't been around to feast on him.

"I'll leave you a moment to collect your thoughts," the big one said. "I'll be in the car."

"Thanks, Nate," Laura said. Then she turned, as if she had only just thought of something. "Actually, Nate? Go on ahead to the motel. I'll walk back. It's not far. I could do with the air."

"Sure thing," Nate said. He turned to walk away, leaving Laura on her own.

Back in his car, the psychic felt a smile curving like the cut of a knife across his face.

The headache was mild, the vision occurring sometime in the far future. He had time. He had plenty of time.

And now he knew.

All he had to do was find Zachary Kingston. Zach was a psychic, too, another target for his list. Laura had revealed as much in that vision. All he had to do was hunt down Zach and kill him, and then he would lure this FBI agent right to him. She would attend his funeral, stand by his grave, and then tell her partner to leave her alone for a while.

There were a lot of things that could happen in a graveyard.

And with enough time to narrow down the location of the cemetery where Zach would be buried – or simply wait until the details were announced – he would be able to check out the routes away from it. He would know which motel, in walking distance, the agent was most likely to stay at – and he could follow her.

Somewhere along the way would be an opportunity. With the two of them in the same town, she would have no chance of seeing him and being able to prepare. She would be defenseless against him. He would take her there – and then he would be invincible. The rest of the psychics of the world would be child's play to take out once he had taken an FBI agent. They would be helpless before him, and he would grow his power to levels that had never before been imagined in his world.

He would be the strongest of them all, and then he would be the last of them all.

There was no point hanging around D.C. The fact that he'd had a vision at all meant that Laura wasn't here, and she was no longer his first target anyway.

He started the engine and began to drive away, heading back to the room he had booked outside of town. He could hole up there, find this Zach and where he lived, and then go right over there to target him.

And before long, Laura Frost would be within his hands as well.

CHAPTER FIFTEEN

Laura winced when Nate put the cell phone to his ear – and she heard Rondelle shouting down the line even from where she sat.

"What do you think you're doing?" Rondelle blustered, and Nate made a face at Laura before replying.

"Sir?" he asked, an obvious and poor attempt to seem innocent.

"I've just had a report cross my desk that you're in some random town in Maryland, requisitioning police resources!" Rondelle said. "Imagine my surprise when I get an identity check to make sure you're genuine agents, for a case I've never even heard of!"

Nate cleared his throat. "I apologize, sir," he said. "We had a lead and we had to come out here to investigate it. We weren't confident that it was a good lead until we checked it out, so we didn't want to waste your time."

"Your time is my time," Rondelle snarled. Laura shifted closer to Nate, ensuring she would still be able to hear both sides of the conversation even if Nate managed to calm Rondelle down. "I pay you, you understand? So if you are wasting your time on some half-baked case, you are wasting my time to begin with!"

"Right," Nate said, somehow managing to come across as contrite and yet stand his ground. "It's just, it's not a waste of time, after all. We've got something here. A serial case – one that hasn't ever been connected before. There's a killer out here that has been flying under the radar for close to a decade."

"And who assigned you to this case?"

Laura felt her heart drop at those words. She knew what they meant. Rondelle wasn't going to allow them to keep investigating. He was going to keep them at headquarters – maybe even send them off out of state on another case. They had challenged his authority by not telling him what they were doing, and he was going to punish them for it – a punishment that would leave the vulnerable women of this town at risk.

"Sir, I'm sorry that we didn't run this by you first," Nate said. "Now that we have established that there is a case, I would be really grateful if you would assign us to it."

"So you want to ask forgiveness, rather than permission, do you?" Rondelle asked. "I'm afraid that's not going to wash. The last thing we need in the Bureau is this kind of maverick behavior. You're not living in a TV show, Lavoie. You have to actually follow the same rules as everyone else. I want you both to get back to Headquarters and stop sticking your noses into cases that aren't yours."

"I understand, sir," Nate said, swallowing hard.

Laura couldn't believe what she was hearing. Was Nate going to just give up, like that? Was he going to leave this town and the people in it, knowing there was only a matter of time before another woman died?

"Right," Rondelle snapped. "Don't let me hear anything about this again."

Nate put the phone down, and Laura looked at him in dismay.

"Don't even say it," he said.

"What?" Laura asked immediately. She spread her hands to either side. "You're just fine with *abandoning* these people -"

"I said, don't say it," Nate said. "You know I'm not."

"Then we have to stay and keep investigating," Laura argued.

"You heard what he said. He wants us back over there."

"No, he wants to not hear about us investigating this case," Laura pointed out. "That's what he said – not to hear about it. He didn't tell us to go back."

"I think his intentions were pretty clear," Nate replied wearily.

"Well, not to me," Laura said. "I didn't even hear the call. I wasn't in the room. So I'm going to carry on."

"Laura…" Nate sighed. He rubbed his hands over his face as if he needed to splash cold water on himself. "Laura, really?"

"What? Are you just going to let a serial killer go because our boss wants us to work on paperwork?" Laura demanded. "Is that why you joined the FBI? To just go where you're told and not actually help people who need you right now?"

"I joined the FBI to catch killers, like you did," Nate muttered. "You know that."

"So how can you just drive away from here and leave it alone, when you know there's one out there, stalking the streets? How are you going to feel when you read the news report about his next victim?"

Silence met Laura's words. For a long moment, she thought she might have gone too far. But then Nate shifted, clearing his throat, and looked at her.

"If we get fired because of this," he said. "You're getting me a new job."

"Absolutely," Laura deadpanned. "I'll set up a psychic private detective agency and you can be my number two. The brawns to my brains."

Nate frowned. "What about my brains?" he asked.

"You won't need them. Easiest job you'll ever work," Laura said. "Deal?"

Nate looked up at the sky. "I must be crazy," he said. "Deal."

Laura smiled. He wasn't crazy. He just knew, like she did, that saving lives was the whole point of the job. And if you weren't saving lives – if you just went on working on other things knowing that you could have saved lives – then what was the point in doing it any longer?

"We need to find out if there's anyone who is connected to all of these bars, preferably someone with a record," Laura said. "Maybe we should check drunk and disorderly records, start there."

"Good idea," Nate said. "Search radius for the last eight years, though? That's going to cause problems. We'll get hundreds, if not thousands, of results."

Laura thought about it. "You're right," she said. "He can't be someone who has so much of a problem with drinking that he can't handle himself. That wouldn't work. Our killer isn't an alcoholic. I think we need some local knowledge, not just police knowledge."

Nate pulled something out of his pocket. "I'll call the manager from the Major Hart and ask."

Laura stared at the piece of paper he was holding. "What is that?" she asked.

"Her number," Nate said. A slow grin crept across his face.

"When did she sneak you that?" Laura exclaimed.

Nate chuckled. "Apparently, I've still got it," he said, putting his cell phone to his ear. A moment later, his tone changed, clearly in response to the call being answered. "Oh, hi – this is Agent Lavoie. We met earlier… Yes, that's right. Look, I was wondering if you could tell me if anyone comes to mind when I give you this description. We're looking for someone who hangs around or used to hang around in the bar, someone who goes to a lot of the bars in town. He wouldn't necessarily be suspicious – just someone who is around a lot."

Laura tuned out Nate's hums of appreciation as the manager replied to him. She got up and went over to the printer, gathering up all the reports they had printed. All these pages of loose paper, signifying the lives of people who had slipped through the cracks. No one had tried to find justice for them yet. Or, at least, they hadn't tried hard enough to make it stick. But that was going to change.

She was going to bring the person who killed these women down – and he was never going to get the chance to do it again. Not while she was here.

She was having the visions for a reason, and she wasn't going to ignore them. What she had said to Nate was absolutely true: They did have a responsibility, something that came along with their badges, to make sure that killers were stopped and caught. Preferably in that order, because it wasn't even really about making arrests or putting people away for life. It was just, when it was all boiled down, about making sure that people weren't murdered.

But above that, above all of it, was something else. Even if Laura hadn't been able to establish a serial killer here by looking at the cases – even if it was two different killers she was pursuing. It didn't matter. What mattered was that her visions had sent her here, and they had sent her here for a reason.

She didn't know why her visions came. She didn't know how to control them. She didn't know why she was the one to get them, and not someone else, or what any of it meant.

But what she did know was that the visions came to her, and she alone had a responsibility to act on them. She alone could see the final moments of these women.

She alone could look into the face of their killer and know, finally, for a fact, that he was the one – and know what his victims had gone through as if she had experienced it herself.

Who else was going to fight harder for them than she would?

"Alright, thanks," Nate was saying. Laura came back over and grabbed a spare folder from the desk that the last occupant had left behind, shoving the printouts inside it. “Yeah, that’s great. No, I definitely will. Alright, bye then.”

“You got something?” Laura asked as he hung up.

“A promise to call back again if I need absolutely anything?” Nate said with his eyes twinkling. “And yes, also, the name of someone we need to talk to. She says he hangs out at the bar sometimes, but she’s seen him at other places too, and he doesn’t really drink much.”

“Someone who spends their time hanging out in bars but doesn’t drink?” Laura frowned.

“Exactly my thoughts,” Nate said, typing rapidly and hitting the enter button on his keyboard. “She said his name is Ellis Long… let me see… ha! He has a record.”

Laura leaned in to see the screen again. “Assault,” she read. “One charge, let off with community service. This could be him.”

“Right?” Nate said. “And the assault charge is nine years ago. Maybe he learned from that time, made sure that the next victim died so there was no one to report him.”

“Maybe,” Laura agreed. “There’s only one way to find out.”

“Let’s go see him,” Nate grinned, hitting print on the page with his address and then shutting the computer down.

CHAPTER SIXTEEN

Nate knew he probably shouldn't say anything. It never went well when he said anything to Laura. She would get defensive and maybe even stop talking to him for a while. She pretty often realized he was right after a certain period of time, but he wasn't sure if now was the right time.

He parked and paused for a moment, looking up at the apartment building. He shot a glance sideways at Laura, wondering.

He was worried about her, but then again, Nate couldn't remember a time in the last few months when he hadn't been worried about her. Longer than that, even. The more he learned about her powers and how hard things truly were for her, the more protective he felt. The more he started to think that she should be sitting safely back at the precinct, or even back in the J. Edgar Hoover Building in D.C., where she couldn't get hurt.

Someone who could do what she did was important. More important than Nate himself, more important than any other agent he'd ever worked with. There was no one else like her, not that he knew. And one day, this reckless way she had was either going to get her killed or fired, and either way, she wasn't going to be able to keep on saving lives the way she did.

"You stay here," Nate tried. "I'll go chat with him."

"Why?" Laura asked. He turned and saw she was giving him a weird look.

"Huh? Well, I just thought it might be better. You stay and keep trying to get a vision about those other cases, so we can get more information."

"Why are you being weird?" Laura asked. "We always go talk to the suspects together."

"Yeah," Nate said. In his head, he was remembering all the times over the years when they'd gone to talk to a suspect together and that suspect had turned out to be violent and aggressive. This one had a track record of violence already, so he wasn't particularly confident that this was going to go calmly.

"Come on, then," Laura said, already getting out of the car.

Nate suppressed a groan and went after her. If he couldn't stop her from putting herself in harm's way, he could at least try and physically put himself between her and it.

"Here," Nate said, finding the intercom button for the name they were looking for – Ellis Long. He pressed the button and held it down for a moment, then let go.

There was a long, awkward silence.

"Try it again?" Laura suggested.

Nate did so, but if the intercom was working, there was no indication. He glanced up at the sky. It was already getting dark – twilight slowly leading the way into night. There was a chance the guy was at work, but only if he was working the night shift.

But, given he was known for enjoying the local nightlife…

"Hey, you looking for someone?"

Nate turned and saw an older woman just walking up towards the apartment building. She looked kind. He made a split-second decision to try to play into that.

"Uh, yeah!" he exclaimed. "Yeah, we're trying to reach Ellis. He lives in the building."

"Oh, Ellis," the old woman said. "I know him. I saw him going out in the direction of The Flagship earlier."

"The Flagship?" Nate asked, exchanging a quick glance with Laura.

"It's a bar, dear," the old woman said, blinking at him. "You go downtown and take a left at the mall, you'll come upon it."

"Thanks," Nate said, grinning, still trying to play the curious friend. "We'll go see if we can catch him, then."

She waved a hand over her head as she shuffled to the lobby doors, and Nate and Laura stepped out of her way. "Have fun," she told them.

Nate looked at Laura and rushed back to the car. If he was in the bar, then it would be a great opportunity to observe him in that environment and see if he did anything suspicious. They were in luck, after all.

"We should try and kind of go undercover and watch him," Nate said, getting back behind the wheel and plugging in his seatbelt. "See what he does."

"I don't know," Laura said. He could feel how eager she was to move on, to solve the case, to get it done. "We don't have hours to spend here. If Rondelle calls and orders us back or we lose our jobs, we don't want to have to tell him all we did was sit in a bar and watch a guy."

"I don't think he'll call tonight," Nate pointed out. "It's getting late. Speaking of, who's paying for the motel tonight?"

Laura sighed deeply. "I guess it's coming out of our own pockets," she said. "It's too far to drive back and forth every morning and night – especially since we've got to finish this before Rondelle snaps, and that could happen at any time. I want to be as close to the town as possible so we can be on the scene as soon as we need to be."

"Scene?" Nate repeated. He risked a glance at her as he pulled out into the road. "You think there's going to be a scene? Like, a new one?"

"I do," Laura nodded. "I can't think of any other reason why I would have these visions – can you? I think he's going to strike again, and we have to stop him before he does that."

"Maybe." Nate bit his lip again, not wanting to say it.

He didn't think they were getting anywhere in particular. Checking out one guy who one bar manager had pinpointed as being kind of odd wasn't a real lead. He knew Laura saw it that way, that she was excited about it. He knew they would have to follow it up, because if they didn't, she was never going to let it drop. She would always be wondering if they had missed the most obvious suspect.

And besides, just because it felt like a reach, didn't necessarily mean Laura was wrong. She'd been right with less to work on before. Nate knew his role in their partnership: to support, to help, to put her in the right places so she could have her visions. To keep her safe between. He wasn't always great at the last part – something he remembered every time she lifted her hand and he saw the burn scars across one side of it – but he did what he could.

"There!" Laura shouted, almost making Nate jerk the wheel to the side and crash the car.

"What? Where?" he demanded, not even sure what he was supposed to be looking for.

"The bar!" Laura exclaimed. "It's right ahead. Here, there's a parking lot – pull in!"

"Okay, wow," Nate said, shaking his head. "You didn't need to give me a heart attack." He pulled in and parked, resting his hands on the steering wheel for a minute, feeling like he needed to catch his breath.

“You need to do more cardio,” Laura said. She turned to get out of the car, leaving Nate to stare after her, speechless. It was only when she leaned down and grinned at him through the window that he realized she was riling him up on purpose.

“I’ll get you for that,” he muttered, which only made her grin more as he got out to join her.

“You sure you don’t want to stay behind for this one?” he asked. “I can bring him out here cuffed, no problem.”

Laura frowned at him, even deeper than she had before. “What’s with you trying to stop me from doing my job today?”

“It’s not that,” Nate said, holding up his hands. “It’s just… are you going to be alright in there?” They’d already visited a bar during this trip, but that had been different. During the day, when the liquor was safely closed up in bottles and taps, not in glasses and ready to be consumed.

“I’ll be fine,” Laura said, turning her back on him and walking towards the doors, conveniently meaning he could no longer see her face.

Nate sighed and followed after her, because there was nothing else he could do.

Inside the bar, the atmosphere was busy. There were people sitting around at tables and on stools at the bar, engaged in spirited conversations. A few televisions high up on the walls were blaring some local sports game, and there was also low-level music piped throughout the place. It was like walking into a wall of sound – almost overwhelming to begin with.

“Great,” Nate muttered. “It’s busy.”

“Well, if he’s a regular, we should be able to narrow it down,” Laura replied, heading towards the bar. She reached for her badge, and Nate was about to put out a hand to stop her and remind her to play it quiet, but her hand moved away on its own. He guessed she had remembered.

“I’ll order us something,” Nate said, gesturing to a couple of seats towards the end of the bar. “Let’s sit and listen.”

Laura opened her mouth but then closed it again, as if she’d thought better of the objection. She sat down at the bar, obediently, and Nate stood by a stool to wait to get the bartender’s attention.

“What can I get you?” he asked, coming closer and wiping his hands on a dish towel over his shoulder.

“Two Cokes,” Nate said. “Do you do food here?”

“We do snacks and bar food,” the bartender replied, reaching for two glasses, and starting to fill one from the tap.

“You have a menu?” Nate asked.

“Sure,” the bartender replied, grabbing a laminated sheet, and passing it over the bar. Nate studied it, tapping his card against the machine when he was prompted. He took a slug of the cold drink, watching Laura do the same from the corner of his eye, and then turned his back against the bar as if he was just settling in.

“What do you think?” he asked.

Laura glanced up from her drink. “I don’t know yet.”

“You want to actually get some food?” Nate asked. “It’s late. Would save us having to grab something at the motel later.”

“If you think it’s a good idea,” Laura said. “What have they got?”

Nate passed the menu over. “Grilled cheese sounds good right about now.”

“Alright, we’ll get two,” Laura said.

“I’m just going to the men’s room,” Nate said. “You know, do a sweep. You order while I’m gone.” He put his drink down on the bar and shoved his hands in the pockets of his black jeans, glad that they had dressed like civilians and not like agents this morning, and walked across the bar.

He looked around with wide swings at first, like he was trying to spot the bathrooms. He spotted them and then did one more sweep before letting his eyes rest on them, just to extend his ability to check out the room.

Once he knew where he was heading there was more opportunity to glance around, always keeping it casual, never lingering on one face for too long. He’d been an FBI agent for a while, after all. He knew how to watch people without letting it seem like he was watching them.

He made it to the bathrooms with a good idea of where everyone was in the room – and with a strong idea of a couple of suspects who fit the description they had been given of Ellis Long.

By the time he’d come back to Laura, with one more sweep across the room, he had narrowed it down to one very likely fit, and that person just happened to have an empty table right beside them.

“Over there,” Nate said, using his head to point as he picked up his drink. “We should go and sit before someone else gets the table.”

Laura looked, nodded, and followed him across the room. Nate kind of hoped those grilled cheeses were still going to be able to find them, because now that he'd thought about food, he was very aware that his stomach was empty.

Laura clocked the guy he thought was Ellis Long immediately – he saw her do it as they sat. The thin, sallow man was seated at a table in the corner on his own, nursing a pint of what looked like soda. He was watching the bar around him, not looking down at a phone or anything else, which made it all the more difficult to surveil him. With proximity, however, Nate was hoping to overhear anything he might say – and maybe even tempt him to engage them in conversation, thinking they were just patrons like him.

"You think he's going to know to bring the grilled cheeses over?" Nate asked, because they had to pretend to engage in normal conversation in order to fool their mark. And, also, yes, because he was hungry.

"I gave him a nod as we moved," Laura said, setting her glass down after another sip. "He knows."

"Good, good," Nate said. "So, uh. How's Lacey doing with school?"

Laura gave him a blank look for a moment, then seemed to look inside herself for a moment as she changed gears. "Yeah, she's doing good. I mean, it's her first proper year of school. It's all new. But it's not like they have big grade milestones to pass yet. I think she's doing fine."

"That's good," Nate nodded. "Does she go to the same school as Amy?"

"No," Laura said, then laughed. "God, no. Marcus has her in a school near his home. Neither of us would be able to afford the school Chris put Amy in."

"She could probably move, though," Nate said, glancing at Laura sideways and keeping Ellis Long in his peripheral vision.

"Why would she move?" Laura asked.

"Because, you know," Nate shrugged. "You and Chris are getting pretty close, I thought. You told him everything and he accepted it, right?"

"Yeah…" Laura frowned, as if she was troubled by what he had said.

"I shouldn't have said anything," Nate backtracked hastily. He didn't actually want to distract her from the task at hand – it was just supposed to be small talk. "I'm sure you guys will figure everything out in your own time. Marcus might not want Lacey to change schools, anyway. I'm babbling."

Laura flashed him a smile. "You are babbling," she agreed.

"Two grilled cheeses," a waitress announced, swooping by their table with two plates. Nate's eyes almost jumped out of his head at the size of the meals: dripping in stringy, hot, melted cheese, they looked just a little like heaven. He was going to have to spend some time in the gym to make up for this, but it looked like it was going to be more than worth it.

"Thanks," Laura said, and Nate mumbled in agreement, unable to take his eyes off the feast that had been set before him. In retrospect, maybe he should have had more than a snack on the road for lunch.

"How you doing, Ellis? Need a top-up?" the waitress asked.

Nate tried very hard not to go still and give the game away.

"Nah, I'm fine," the man at the table behind them said.

Nate smiled at his grilled cheese. He'd been right. That was Ellis Long. Now they had his identity confirmed, the only thing left to do was watch his behavior.

Nate grabbed one half of his sandwich and took a healthy-sized bite, almost rolling his eyes back into his head at the flavor. He tasted at least three types of cheese, and the bread was soaked in butter before it was grilled – he could sense just how much.

It was so good, he almost forgot for a minute that they were there to do a job, not just to have dinner.

"This is so good," he said out loud, knowing again that it was a good idea to keep acting normal and having a conversation. People didn't just sit in silence when they were having dinner together, not unless there was some serious source of awkwardness between them.

"Yeah, it's really nice," Laura said, but he noticed she was only picking at it.

"You want to order anything else?" he asked. "I mean, we could get fries or something to go with it?"

"No, no," Laura sighed, taking another bite as if to prove that she was fine. "This is good. You're right."

Nate felt like he was being pulled in too many directions. There was the grilled cheese, which his stomach and tongue loudly demanded he pay attention to, since it was both necessary and delicious. There was Laura, who seemed to be struggling a little – and he hoped it wasn't because of what he had said about Chris.

And there was Ellis Long, sitting in silence right by them, who was too observant to be observed and yet wasn't doing anything to give them more of an in.

Nate took a few more bites in silence, hyper alert to everything around them. A couple from a nearby table got up and left. He glanced around at the other patrons of the bar, wondering if there was anyone who fit Long's type, but there didn't seem to be any drunk women on their own. Then again, if they were alone when they left, that was a different issue.

Then another movement to the side caught Nate's attention, and he realized very fast that it was the worst possible thing.

Ellis Long was leaving the bar.

CHAPTER SEVENTEEN

Laura looked up and felt her heart drop at the fact that Ellis Long was standing up, picking up his coat from the chair beside him and putting it on.

He was leaving.

She glanced at Nate.

"Do you want to go?" Nate asked, which was about as clear as he could be without actually saying it out loud.

Laura didn't answer him; there wasn't time. He'd made it clear that he would go with her decision. She turned instead, as if she was just casually trying to get someone's attention.

"Ellis Long?" she asked, in a voice that was low enough for only him to hear it. The less of a fuss they caused here, the better.

He nodded, frowned, and looked at her with what she could only describe as the deepest possible level of distrust.

"Could we have a chat?" she asked. The table that Nate had chosen had four chairs, and they were only taking up two of them. "You can have a seat."

"Who are you?" Long responded, his frown deepening further.

"It's just an informal chat," Laura said. And she took a chance, because she couldn't see any other way to get him to sit down at the table and talk to them. She showed him her badge.

"What the hell?" Long exploded, his voice loud enough to make several people around them turn and stare. "Is this some kind of entrapment?"

"No, it's an informal chat," Laura said, trying to remain outwardly calm as her heart pounded in her chest. In her head, she began running scenarios. The worst case would be if everyone else in the bar was pro-Ellis Long and anti-FBI, and things turned violent. "We're just here having dinner, and I happened to overhear your name. Well, we're in town taking a review of a couple of cold cases, so we just wanted to check up on whether you had given a witness statement to the initial investigation."

"Well, I can answer that for you right now," he snorted. "I've never given a witness statement to any investigation. Now, I'm leaving."

"Just hold on," Nate said, holding out a hand as Ellis Long tried to pass by. "We'd like you to make one if it's not too much trouble. It's very simple. A few yes or no answers. It won't take up much of your time."

"I'm not letting you do some fit-up job on me," Long snarled, backing away.

"I really think it's a good idea that you have just an informal chat with us now," Laura said. There was a fine line between spooking him and making him feel like it was in his best interests to stay, and she was losing confidence that she could walk that line. "I don't want to have to do this down at the local precinct, and neither do you."

"Screw you, pigs," he snarled, and made a move towards the exit.

He was quick, but Nate was quicker. Within seconds he was up, blocking Long's way to the exit, a bodily presence that might as well have been a wall. Laura stood up to give him back-up from the other side, leaving Long with nowhere to run to.

"I'm going to have to ask you to come down to the precinct with us," Nate said.

That was when Ellis Long made the stupidest mistake of his life.

He tried to shove Nate, a man who was easily twice his weight in muscle alone, in the chest to get him to move aside.

Nate simply stared back at him.

"Move out of the damn way," Long snarled, shoving him harder and then raining down a couple of blows from closed fists on Nate's chest.

Laura could see this getting heated, especially with an audience. A quick glance around showed that several of the locals were clearly interested in what was going on, and some of them were setting down their glasses as if gearing up to wade in. She stepped forward quickly, taking out a pair of handcuffs – thankful to herself for bringing them, when she wasn't properly kitted up as she would have been on a normal case – and grabbed one of his wrists. He flailed but she managed to get it hooked on, and Nate grabbed the other wrist so she could get the cuffs connected.

"Alright," Laura said quietly, trying to keep things simple and isolated to just the three of them. "That's enough. You're coming down to the precinct to answer some questions, on suspicion of murder. Got that?"

Long's only answer was to struggle so hard against his cuffs that he nearly fell over and took her out with him. She made a desperate sound and righted him again, and Nate grabbed his lapel to stop him falling a second time.

"Hey," someone said, standing up from a nearby table – a tall, older man with a long straggling beard who looked like he had seen a fight or two in his life. "What do you want with Ellis?"

"This matter doesn't concern you, sir," Laura said, wanting to get Long out of there before things reached a tipping point. She and Nate were only two.

"I think it does," the man said, and another couple of men from the same table stood up, folding their arms across their chest. Laura was beginning to get the impression that although Long was regarded as a local weirdo, he was seen as *their* weirdo. In the sense that it was quite possible half the town would show up in his defense if they thought that outsiders were targeting him.

Laura looked around and realized that a lot of eyes were turned their way. Feeling the need to prevent some kind of challenge going any further – and especially the risk of them being overpowered by the crowd - she lifted up her badge and showed it to the room at large. "This situation is under control," she said. "We're actively seeking information in the murders of Joy Kingsley and July Hall. If any of you have information, I would urge you to come forward." That, she hoped, was enough of an announcement to diffuse things – the implications being twofold: first, that Long was being arrested for the murders, and second, the same awaited anyone else who kept information to themselves.

She turned, giving Nate a look which she hoped he would interpret as a need for haste, and started to hustle Long out of the bar. They needed to get going before someone decided that they didn't like the FBI very much anywhere and were happy to risk getting thrown in cuffs themselves in order to make a point. Thankfully, perhaps because of the speed with which they moved, no one followed them – except for the eyes of just about everyone in the place.

It was only when they were right at the door that she caught Nate looking back longingly at the table and the remains of the grilled cheese he hadn't been able to finish.

"Cheer up," she told him as they stepped into free air and headed rapidly towards the car. "If we just caught a murderer, I'll buy you takeout."

***

Laura groaned, leaning back in her chair and then immediately sitting straight again in response to the uncomfortable, stiff structure. It was worse than sitting in a school chair. "We need to get him to talk," she said.

"Yeah, but I don't see how we're going to do that," Nate said. "He's given us that no-comment bull at least fifty times. And now that he's refusing to talk without a lawyer, we don't have a choice."

"As soon as a lawyer gets here, he's just going to tell his client not to say a single word," Laura pointed out. "If we had DNA from either of the victims we would be able to compare it to his, but there's nothing. The man I saw doing this – he was wearing gloves, a coat and hoodie covering his hair. He knew what he was doing. There's not going to be any DNA unless we find some kind of early case where he messed up."

Nate grimaced and shook his head. "This sucks. And I'm hungry. You promised me takeout."

"I promised you takeout if we had a killer, which we still don't know for sure," Laura pointed out. She sighed and checked her watch. If she had been at home, she would have been in bed by now, never mind dinner. "But, fine. Go order something. I don't care what."

"Alright!" Nate grinned, practically leaping out of his chair and heading out into the hall.

Laura stayed where she was. She needed to keep an eye on Ellis Long. They'd left him in the interview room while they waited for this elusive lawyer to show up. He was sitting in his chair – a very similar one to the torture device she was sitting on, which made her feel somewhat better – with his arms folded across his chest, not moving. She tried to picture the face of the killer in her visions, obscured and half-seen in the dark as it was, fitting it against his face. Was he the same man? Could that be the same nose she had seen, the same eyes?

It was almost impossible. She sighed, knowing that she wasn't going to get anywhere by just going over it again and again in her own head. She needed another vision. Another clue of some kind.

Something that would take her over the edge and let her know that she was on the right path.

The whole while they had been arresting Long, all the time she'd had his arm in her hand, the march from the car to the precinct, all of it – she hadn't had a single vision. Didn't that mean something? Was she barking up the wrong tree?

The door opened and Laura looked up, expecting to see Nate asking her to choose between takeout options – but it wasn't him at all. It was one of the local police officers who had assisted them since they came into the precinct, a man whose name Laura had already forgotten.

"Hi, Agent Frost? We just heard from the lawyer that represents Long. He's not going to be here until the morning. I told him we'd have to hold his client until he gets here, and he just said something about it adding to the official complaint he was going to be filing as soon as he arrives."

Laura groaned, rubbing her forehead. "Fine. Take him to the holding cells for the night, then," she said. "He can decide for himself whether he thinks his lawyer is a brilliant strategist or should be fired for calling our bluff and making him sleep here."

"Right," the officer nodded, quickly disappearing, and closing the door. Laura got the impression that she was coming across as being in a bad mood, and the man had wanted to get away from her so she couldn't take it out on him.

Which was fine, because being alone suited her perfectly just then.

Idly, because she had nothing better to do, she started to search for Ellis Long on social media. One of his accounts came up with very little in the way of posts – it seemed like he sporadically put up a stylistic shot of a glass of whisky around Christmas each year, or a dark and moody self-portrait on his birthday – no doubt a way to fish for wishes from those who wouldn't otherwise have known it was that date. The rest was very much of the character she expected from him: a shot of a night sky with leafless branches intersecting it, a dark and grainy shot of the outside of a museum, and so on.

There were very few shots with friends or even family members, that much she noticed right away.

She scrolled back further, and as the years passed by in just a handful of posts each time, she quickly found herself stumbling on a richer vein of images. These were posted much closer together in terms of dates, and they were brighter. There were even shots of Long with friends – and with a beautiful young woman who caught Laura's eye.

She tapped on the post to open it, and found a caption about celebrating an anniversary with the woman he loved – something almost poetic in its romance, and definitely at odds with the man she saw in front of her now. Laura saw the date under the post – three years ago – and bit her lip. She started to scroll up slowly, reading every post, looking for the moment that everything had changed.

But there was a moment before that which made her stop, almost dropping her phone at the sight of it. A post about how they had just landed in beautiful Rome, Italy, for a two-week vacation.

And the date at the bottom of the post was a week before July Hall had been murdered.

Which meant…

Laura carried on scrolling, biting her lip harder now. The next post had Ellis and the smiling woman exploring ancient Roman ruins; there was another shot of them sitting in a café which was juxtaposed next to a rack of Italian newspapers and magazines bearing headlines about a certain American president, all of which had dates fully visible. The day after July Hall had been found.

Laura sank her head into her hands.

Whatever Ellis Long was – whatever he had been through – he wasn't the killer they were looking for. He couldn't be. He had a foolproof alibi. She had no idea why he had refused to answer their questions – perhaps he was just affronted by the way they had approached him, or perhaps whatever it was that had darkened his outlook on life had also made him resentful of law enforcement – but it wasn't him.

Nate opened the door and came in with the phone pressed to his ear, and Laura didn't even have the energy to look up.

"Yes, sir, I'm with her now," Nate said.

And Laura found that she did have the energy to look up – in alarm.

"Yes. Yes, I know that you asked us to stop investigating," Nate said. "We had a very strong feeling about this suspect, and we have reason to believe we may well have solved the case. We were so close."

Laura made a quick gesture with her hands, slicing them across the top of one another. *Stop*. Nate faltered, clearly trying to interpret her message.

"Yes… yes, sir, I do understand. No, it wasn't a bar fight – he just resisted a little. No, we had it under control right away. No, sir. Not a single punch." Nate paused, listening. "Tomorrow morning. Yes, sir. I do understand. And that's completely fair about the motel and food. Yes, absolutely, we'll leave it in the hands of the locals once it's all wrapped up. Okay… Yes, sir."

He looked down at his phone all of a sudden, and from the blank screen, Laura could guess that he had been hung up on.

"What did he say?" Laura asked, knowing full well it must have been Chief Rondelle on the other end of the line.

"He said we have until tomorrow to wrap the case up now that we've arrested a suspect," Nate said. "And also that he's not paying for the motel or any food and drink reimbursements. I didn't ask him about the gas, but I'm guessing you won't be getting reimbursed for that, either."

"I don't care," Laura said irritably. "It's just gas. But I wish you hadn't gone so hard on reassuring him about our suspect."

A look of horror came over Nate's face. "No," he said.

"I'm afraid so," Laura said. She turned her own cell phone in his direction so he could see the post, feeling like she wanted to go lie down in a dark room on her own for about three years.

"Oh, man," Nate said. "Now I wish I hadn't said all that, too. I'm going to sound like an idiot when I have to tell him we let the guy go."

"Being an idiot is the best you can hope for at this point," Laura said. "Being an idiot means he just tells us to come back home and gives us the worst jobs for a few months until he gets over it. Being an idiot means we're still working for the FBI."

Nate gave her a look – a Look with a capital L.

"I told you if I lost my job over this…"

"I know, I know," Laura sighed. "I owe you a psychic private detective agency. But you also can't honestly tell me that your conscience would have let you go back and forget about this case if we really were that close to catching the killer."

Nate nodded ruefully. "If we lose our jobs, it's as much my fault as yours," he said. "I shouldn't try and put this all on you. You're right. I agreed to stay. And I did it for exactly the reasons you're saying. This isn't just a job for us; it's the right thing to do."

"Now all we have to do is find a new suspect and confirm them as the killer before, oh, ten in the morning tomorrow?" Laura said. "You know. No pressure."

She reached for her cell phone, thinking about the next phase of research, but as she did so a headache spiked into her head. She grabbed it up ready to turn the screen on, waiting for the –

Lacey and Amy were sitting together in a room. A familiar room. Lacey's room at Laura's apartment. Everything was as Laura had left it – the same toys on the bed, the same drawings on the walls. Nothing had changed. That meant it had to be happening soon.

The two girls were sitting together on the bed – and hugging one another, both of them looking anxiously towards the door.

"I don't like the bad man," Lacey whispered. "He's scary."

"It's okay," Amy said, though Laura could see she was just as scared as her slightly younger friend. "Uncle Chris will come here to get me soon. He'll come and help."

"And Mommy will stop the bad man," Lacey replied. Laura's heart was breaking. She could see that even though her little girl was saying the words, she was no longer sure that she believed them. She wanted them to be true, but she was so afraid. "That's my Mommy's job. She told me. She catches bad men and stops them from being bad all the time."

Something – Laura couldn't see or hear what – made the girls jump, and then –

Laura blinked, her mind and her lungs filling with searing white-hot panic.

"What is it?" Nate asked. "Did you see something?"

Laura couldn't answer him. Her hands shook as she tried to open her phone's calling menu, fumbling twice, and having to start again, finding Chris's number and hitting dial. She pressed a hand to her chest, feeling her breathing coming sharp and quick, her heart pounding out a drumbeat she couldn't even measure. The girls were in danger.

The girls were in danger.

"Hey, Laura," Chris said. "You're lucky. I was just going to bed."

"Chris," Laura gasped out, hanging onto the edge of the desk like it was a life raft. "Chris, where are the girls?"

"The girls?" Chris repeated, as if he didn't understand the question. "Amy's tucked up in bed. I'm guessing that Lacey is with Marcus."

"She's safe?" Laura asked. "Chris, go check on her. Go make sure she's in bed."

"Okay," Chris said, his voice strange. "Alright, just give me a minute."

The line went quiet.

"What's going on?" Nate hissed quietly beside her.

Laura waved a hand in his direction, needing him to shut up. She couldn't handle everything at once right now. She couldn't.

"She's asleep," Chris said, his voice low as he no doubt crept away from Amy's room, trying not to wake her. "Do you want to tell me what this is about?"

"I saw something," Laura said, drawing in a shuddering breath. She was still shaking, unable to stop. "I saw the two of them locked up together in Lacey's room at my place. They were afraid of something. A – a bad man that they were hoping I would protect them from. And you."

Nate sucked in a breath beside her.

"What does that mean?" Chris asked. She could hear him pacing backward and forward, probably in the kitchen from the sound of the room. "When is this going to happen?"

"I don't know," Laura said. She buried her head in her free hand for a moment. "I don't know, I don't know. And it doesn't have to happen. If we can stop it – if we can work out what it means before it gets that far, it won't come true."

"Then what does it mean?" Chris asked. She could hear the tension rising in his voice as well, the panic that she felt herself.

"I don't know," Laura replied. She was on the verge of hyperventilating. "This aura of – of danger that I sensed around you – it's on Nate, too. And now this thing with the girls – I think something is coming. Something that we're all going to be involved in. Something that could put all of us in danger."

"Except for you, right?" Chris said. "You haven't seen anything about yourself?"

"Why would I?" Laura asked. "I can't sense an aura around myself. And seeing the girls – they were in my place. Why would they be in my place if I wasn't caught up in it?"

Chris took a breath. "Alright, look – you say they were together in your vision?"

"Yes," Laura said, squeezing her eyes tight shut as she remembered how scared they had looked, how they had clutched onto one another.

"Then it's simple. We keep them apart," Chris said. "As long as you're away, Amy will stay with me and Lacey is with her dad, anyway. And when you're back, we just have to make sure the two of them aren't together until we get to the bottom of this. If they aren't together, then what you saw can't happen. I'll see if I can stay home for a few days, or maybe take Amy to visit with my mom and dad for the rest of the week. That way, she's far away from here and absolutely safe, and if Lacey's far away from her, then Lacey is safe too."

"Okay," Laura nodded. "Okay, yes. Do that."

"Will it work?" Chris asked, and when Laura realized that the confidence he'd been projecting had unstable ground, she felt it crumbling beneath her feet as well.

"It will keep Amy safe," Laura said, and she found her throat choking, closing up, thinking of Lacey alone in that bedroom with no one to cling onto, no one to keep her safe. "I… I'll make sure Marcus keeps Lacey for a while. I won't have her over on weekends until it's over. Like you said, if they're far away from the place where I saw them, they should be safe."

"Alright," Chris said, and breathed heavily. "Christ, Laura."

"I'm sorry," Laura said, the word coming out half as a sob, feeling like she was the one who had brought all of this on them. She would never give up her power so long as it was keeping the people she loved safe – but there were times when selfishly, cowardly, she almost wished she didn't have to be the one to know.

"We'll get through this, whatever it is," Chris said. "We'll keep the girls safe. That's what matters most of all. And as soon as it's over, we can all be together again. As soon as we know that they're safe."

"Okay," Laura said, hoarsely, her voice barely above a whisper. She cleared her throat. "I'd better go. We're still on this new case."

"Alright," Chris said. "Be safe, Laura."

"You too," she said, hanging up and dropping her head into both hands this time. She felt the heavy warmth of Nate's reassuring hand on her back, but it didn't take away the fear of what she had seen. The fear of something happening to her daughter.

"What do you want to do now?" Nate asked, and there were so many things swirling around in Laura's head that for a moment, she couldn't even conceive of an answer.

CHAPTER EIGHTEEN

Hayley stumbled a little as she walked away from the bar, cursing her stupid heels and her stupid drunk feet and her stupid sense of balance. She shrugged her zipped hoodie higher up on her shoulders and threw the hood over her head, grabbing the material tighter around her body as she started to walk.

She wasn't supposed to be walking. She hadn't planned on walking. But the stupid bouncer had told her she was too drunk to drive and had taken her stupid car keys when she got them out, and had insisted on telling her to call a cab or let him do it for her. And she hadn't wanted to explain to him that she couldn't afford a damn cab. She couldn't afford a damn drink, but it was the only thing that got her through the week. The last thing she could manage was a cab on top of all the extra drinks she shouldn't have had.

Not that she had paid for all of them. Hayley swung her long, dark hair over her shoulders, nearly toppling over with the extra sway it gave her, pursing and then parting her perfectly glossed lips as if blowing a kiss to some invisible person in the distance. She had done pretty well tonight. She could have had her choice of men to go home with.

Only, she didn't want to go home with any men. She wanted to go home on her own. So now she was stuck walking because she wasn't allowed to drive her own damn car, and she couldn't afford a stupid taxi.

Hayley shoved her hands into the pockets of her hoodie, scowling at everyone and everything, even though the whole road in front of her was basically deserted.

At least it was a quiet back road she was walking down. She wouldn't have to deal with cat calls for the short shorts she'd gone out in tonight, paired with the kind of shoes that were usually referred to as stripper heels. Hayley had the ability to balance well in really, stupidly tall shoes, so she wasn't going to waste it – not when men seemed to enjoy it so much.

But there were times when you didn't want that kind of attention, and trying to walk home in the middle of the night was one of them.

Hayley wasn't dumb enough to accept a ride from some stranger pulling up alongside her. No way. Back here, no one was going to bother her, so she could just focus on getting back home quickly.

She did sort of wish there were streetlights along the route, but her eyes were starting to adjust now anyway, so it was going to be fine.

Hayley stopped walking for a moment to reach down and adjust one of the straps on her left ankle, and when the clattering of her heels stopped for a moment – she heard it.

A footstep.

She turned quickly, dark hair whipping around behind her. She almost went over onto the sidewalk, instead awkwardly moving from a flamingo pose to crouching on all fours, one of her hands still on the buckle. It was in the right place now, anyway. There was a man behind her.

He was a ways down the road, like he had left the bar a couple of minutes after she had. She could have sworn he had stopped walking when she did, only dropping that one footstep, like it was a mistake and he hadn't meant to be heard.

But now he was walking on towards her again, and even in her present state, a spike of fear cut right through the alcohol and deep into Hayley's brain.

There was a man following her. And whether he was deliberately following her, or just coincidentally taking the same route, they were alone on the road together in the dark. Hayley knew enough to know that there was no way she could be sure this situation was safe, and that meant she had to get out of it as soon as she could.

She stood up straight and started moving, focusing on putting one foot in front of the other. When she focused like this, she could manage to go pretty fast, even when drunk. The alcohol was starting to siphon off a little bit now that she was realizing that she was in a serious situation. The cold was helping, too. The shoes were tall, but the sidewalk was flat and straight, and she knew this area well, and if all she needed to do was walk then she could put all her energy into it.

Hayley walked as fast as she could for a long stretch, for as long as she could bear, without getting an update on how close he was, and then she risked her balance for a moment to look behind her.

He wasn't there.

At least, not within the range of her vision – because she could only see so far in the dark. And if he was far enough behind her that she could no longer see him…

She had effectively lost him.

Hayley gave a chuckle of relief out loud to herself, allowing her pace to drop just a little. Not so much that he would have a chance to catch up again, since that would be stupid. She let herself relax a bit, looking to the side at all the new-build homes that were slowly going up there. She remembered walking along this road when there was literally nothing on either side. She remembered seeing the foundations being dug. It was kind of exciting now, seeing that they were almost completed, thinking of the people who would be moving in soon.

She followed the curve of the road as it bent around the new development, glancing over her shoulder one more time at the apex and still seeing nothing. She really had lost him. She was alone on the road again.

Which left her remembering it was pretty cold, wrapping her hoody tighter about herself over her low-cut top. Soon she would be home, she told herself, and there was a big old duvet waiting for her along with some pajamas that would have made her grandmother proud.

Hayley looked up from concentrating on her feet to see how far she had left to go, and her steps faltered.

He was there – ahead of her. She was sure it was still him by the outline of his shape, the silhouette she had seen behind her. A hood up over his head, an overcoat that hung partway down his calves. That was him.

He must have gone around through the development – cut his way along the other side of the new lots there. He'd cut out the bend and got there way ahead of her.

And now he was just standing there, right in the middle of the path where she needed to go, watching her. She couldn't even see his face, but somehow, she just knew. He was watching.

Hayley stopped walking altogether, and for a moment the two of them just stared at one another in silence.

Then he took his hands out of his pockets and started to walk towards her, and Hayley had never known so much fear in her life.

She turned and ran, relying on her muscle memory to keep her upright and not let her trip in the heels, wishing they weren't attached by straps so she could kick them off, wishing she wasn't drunk, wishing she had just called a taxi.

Hayley ran and ran, until the inevitable happened and she tripped, going down hard and only at the last minute having enough presence of mind and control to pitch herself to the side so that she rolled onto the grass embankment instead of skinning her legs and hands.

She rolled and put herself onto her back, the best way she could think of to be able to see how close he was and to try to get back onto her feet, but there he was – right in front of her. She looked to the side, looked around desperately for something to grab that she could use to defend herself. Her cell phone had fallen out of her pocket, fallen onto the sidewalk. She lunged for it –

But he was on her already, strong hands grabbing her and shoving her back, putting her where she had started. She spared one last glance for the phone that could have been her lifeline and then up at him, and the way he smiled at her made her heart beat so fast in terror she thought she might die right there and then.

He muttered something she couldn't make out and brought his hand down towards her head, and the last thing she knew was a pain in her temple and complete blackness as unconsciousness swallowed her whole.

CHAPTER NINETEEN

Laura lay on the motel's stiff and uncomfortable bed, trying to ignore the scratchiness of the sheets. She rolled over again, trying to get comfortable.

There was no getting comfortable.

Not when she knew full well there was a killer still out there, thinking he'd got away with it all, believing no one even knew his victims were linked.

Two year gaps between cases, and the last one was two years ago. There was no way of telling when he would strike again. It could be today. It could be next week. It could be three or four months from now – or he could already have attacked and killed someone who had fallen off the radar.

Laura rolled again and then gave up, sitting up in bed with a sigh.

She needed to get deeper into the killer's mind. That was always what helped. The more she got into their minds, knew how they thought, the better she was at tracking them down and knowing where they would go next. Not only was that just the standard way it worked for any FBI agent, but it would also help her to have more visions, to be able to interpret them better.

The problem was that she kept having her visions when she was asleep. That was why she had suggested to Nate that they take a break for the night, at a time when she would normally have been dead set on staying up and investigating until dawn broke and beyond. She would normally have thought that sleep was useless right now, and investigating was the only thing that could pull them forwards.

But these days, it turned out, she was doing a lot of investigating in her dreams, as weird as that was.

In order to do that, of course, she actually had to fall asleep – which was proving impossible with all the turmoil her thoughts were in.

Laura pressed her hands against her temple, resting her elbows on her knees so that she was fully supported, trying to relax as well as to think. Getting stressed out about everything – including the safety of her daughter and the other people she loved – wasn't helping. If anything, it was making things worse, because the more she worried, the less she slept.

She needed to find some way to calm herself. Some way to focus in on the killer. To be him. To understand how he felt, what he saw, how it moved him to act.

She closed her eyes and focused, going over the first vision she had seen in as much detail as she could manage. She allowed herself to really linger there, to be part of it again. To see the lights of the bar shining on Joy's hair as she moved away from it. To see the way she stumbled slightly and swayed from time to time. The way her eyes changed when she thought someone was behind her.

Laura focused on every small detail, replaying it as closely as she could to the original, absorbing herself back into the vision like she was watching it at the theater, letting it take up the whole of the screen in her mind, filling everything she could see. Every time she thought of Lacey or Nate or Chris, or Rondelle and the time pressure she was under, she pushed it aside and tried to get back to where she had been. To let the moment linger even longer in recompense. To be part of it as much as she could.

The forest where Joy Kingsley had run was empty. There was no one around to disturb the peace of the night. Somewhere, a night bird called. There was a rustling underfoot here and there from the smallest of animals moving in the undergrowth. In the middle of it all, the hut: alone and abandoned. It was derelict, the door snapped in half. No one slept there tonight, lured by the scant shelter it could provide, hardly anything against the elements and the cold of February.

Wind shuffled the loose boards, creaked through the open windows that hadn't seen glass in a long time, moved the stems of the weeds that had grown up close around the hut's exterior. It was quiet here, deathly quiet. But still, somehow, there was a sense that the place was waiting. That someone would be back. That it wasn't over.

A sense that –

Laura's eyes snapped open as she sat up straight, blinking in the dim light of the room. She hadn't even noticed when she had slipped into the vision, when the line between memory and imagination and then the vision itself had been drawn. It was like she had gone there again, back to the place they had already visited in search of the killer, the place where he had killed Joy Kingsley.

Laura wiped a hand over her face, feeling surprisingly drained. It had been like watching a video link directly to the spot. Being there without being there. It was the weirdest vision she had ever had, by far. Was it even a vision? Or was she… what? Telepathically spying on specific places now? Was that a thing?

Laura lay back down on the pillows with a groan. How did that even help her? She was supposed to be trying to have a vision of one of the killings so that she could study the man who was doing all of this, and maybe even get a proper glimpse of his face that she could memorize. Not just randomly jumping around to different places to unlock new facets of her power that she didn't know she had – least of all how to use them.

This whole thing was a waste of time, as usual when she tried to make her psychic abilities actually work with her.

If they were a person, they would be the most stubborn person she had ever met. Someone who only wanted to work when they weren't being told to.

She closed her eyes and flung an arm across her forehead to try to keep them shut, thinking now that the only possible way she could ever manage to get anywhere on this case before dawn would be a real vision – and that the only way that would come would be if she was really asleep.

***

Laura felt like hell when her alarm went off, blaring into the still-dark room at the break of dawn. She cracked the motel room blinds just enough to spot the first glimmer of light on the horizon and then begrudgingly dressed and prepared herself, getting ready for the day ahead.

Or the morning ahead, really. Because now they only had around six hours to try to get this case solved and closed before Rondelle would be screaming for their heads on spikes. Six hours left to save their careers as FBI agents.

What a stark contrast, Laura could only think, from the way he treated them when they came back from a case with the right results. She knew Rondelle had a lot of pressure on him to make sure all his agents – and he controlled hundreds of them directly – were operating at the highest possible level. But a little bit of trust for the two agents he himself claimed were his best… was that really too much to ask?

There was a light knock on Laura's door, three taps with a kind of rolling motion that was designed to get her attention without waking up anyone else who might be sleeping in the complex. Laura grabbed her cell phone, the last thing she needed, and headed over to open the door, seeing Nate ready to go right outside.

"Hey," he whispered. "You ready?"

"I'm ready," she said, shrugging her FBI-branded windbreaker on over her shoulders. There was no point in being subtle today. After the encounter with Ellis Long in a very public place last night, there was little hope that anyone would be unaware of who they were – especially anyone who spent time in the town's nightlife and would hear the conversations going around the bars. Today she was wearing the black suit, the windbreaker, and her badge on her belt. Today, they were going out in force.

It was the only card they had left to play.

They moved to the car in silence, and it was only when they were seated and Nate had his hands on the wheel that he looked over at her and asked. "Where do you want to start today? Did you get anything last night?"

"I just had a vision of the place where we went first," Laura said. "The hut in the woods. I don't know that it even means anything."

"Alright," Nate said thoughtfully. "Well, I figure if we can't get help from your visions, then we go back to old-fashioned police work."

"My thoughts exactly," Laura agreed. "Let's set up at the precinct again and start from there."

"Rondelle will hear about it if we use their resources," Nate pointed out.

"He already knows we're here," Laura shrugged. "I don't know how much worse it could get."

"Good point," Nate said, though he sounded uncomfortable with it. "I think we need to dig into the data we have from these five victims. Like you said, it gives us a pattern to work with. We need to find out everything we can about that pattern. If we can't identify who he is, maybe we can at least identify when and where he's likely to strike again."

"I like that idea," Laura nodded. The precinct loomed up ahead, and Nate slowed the car to turn into the parking lot. "I want to look at it from all angles. Geography, calendar, victimology, everything."

"We'll go through it all bit by bit," Nate said. He parked up and looked at her. "But we have to do it fast. Only a few hours and then we're going to hit Rondelle's deadline."

"And if we don't meet it?" Laura asked, voicing a fear that she was already harboring.

Nate went silent for a moment, looking out of the windshield at the parked cars around them. Laura had the impression that he wasn't seeing any of them at all. "We'll cross that bridge when we come to it," he said at last, taking off his seatbelt.

They got out of the car and walked into the precinct, earning more than a few open stares. Laura figured that Rondelle had called and spoken to their chief, who of course had let it leak that their boss was none too happy with them. They had all probably expected that, since they'd let their last suspect go, they wouldn't be around today. Whether their determination to continue despite the odds made them good agents or just stupid remained to be seen.

"Hi," Laura said, addressing the very first detective they walked past. "I need a map of the town. Something that includes the outskirts. And physical, not something online. I need to pin it up and mark things on it."

"Right," he nodded. He looked just nonplussed enough to go and do what she asked without questions, which was perfect.

Laura and Nate headed straight for the same desks they had been working at the day before, finding them still unoccupied. That was good, at least. Having to move around and find a new base was tedious. She took the folder full of printed case files she had created yesterday out from under her arm and placed it on the desk, starting to gather each of the sets of pages into piles so they could go through them one by one.

The detective she had spoken to materialized with a map of the area, crisply folded and clearly unused. At her gestured direction, he spread it out across the empty space on the desk, allowing them to see the whole of the town and its environs at a glance.

"Thanks," Laura said, then turned to Nate. "Right."

"I'm ready," Nate said, holding up a tub of pushpins and a red marker pen he must have procured from someone else while she was busy and not paying attention.

Laura grinned. It was good to work with someone who always understood exactly what she wanted to do. "First victim, chronologically. Allison Park. She was found in the forest – roughly opposite to Westfield Lane on the west side of town; you should be able to find a clearing."

Nate studied the map with a frown. "I have something – it's marked with the symbol for a ruined structure."

"That's right," Laura nodded. "According to this, there was a ruined building – the remains of an old forester's hut – that was being used by homeless people. Someone had put up a tarp over it. That's where she was found – under the tarp."

"Let me guess, they assumed a homeless guy got high and murdered her and then never bothered to fully investigate it," Nate said, his voice almost a growl.

"Sounds like that's about right," Laura agreed. "Mark that with a pin."

Nate pushed the pin into the spot. It gave a little into the desk below, but they could worry about being charged for property damage later. They were already in so much trouble with Rondelle, a little more barely seemed to matter.

"Next was Sarina Waterman in the alleyway by the disused buildings," Laura said, skimming through the report to see if there was anything that would help them narrow the location down further. "Off Buckfield Avenue."

"Hang on," Nate said, doing a search on his cell phone for the location. Once he'd found it, he compared the two maps and then pushed a pin into their paper copy just north of the previous one. "Okay, next?"

"Alayna Honeysett was by the roadside – on the 75, there's a road bridge that goes over a small river."

"I've got it," Nate said, nodding and marking it off in the north of the town.

"Joy Kingsley," Laura said, and didn't have to say anything else as Nate marked off a location that was further to the east – the spot they had driven to when this all started.

"And the last one is July Hall, right?" Nate said.

"Right," Laura confirmed. "Near the warehouses in the south-east."

Nate found and marked the spot off perfectly, given that they were already familiar with the location.

They both stared down at the map.

"Are you seeing what I'm seeing?" Nate asked.

"It's a circle," Laura said. "He's working his way around the outskirts of town."

"And he's doing it by finding all the abandoned spots, places where no one would notice someone," Nate pointed out. "Old ruins, abandoned huts, empty warehouses – it's all places that have been left alone for long enough you could be confident you wouldn't be disturbed. Even the road bridge – once you're underneath it, no one is going to see you from the road."

"It's more than that," Laura said, inspiration striking. "Look. The forester's hut had been made livable with the use of a tarp. We know people have been living in the other hut where Joy was found. You could easily camp under the bridge. No one would notice you sleeping in an empty warehouse. I think he's not just killing them there – I think he's living there. That's why he has to move on to a new spot each time."

"That's why the bars change, but there's overlap in the patrons," Nate mused. "You just have to be walking home along the route near to where he's living. He has all the time in the world to stand there and watch the road at night and wait for someone to come by. He might even be doing it to keep himself safe, given the environment, not specifically to watch for someone to kill."

"But then he sees her, and he can't resist," Laura said. "It's been a couple of years since the last one. He remembers what it was like. The rush of power. The way he felt when he saw the life go out of their eyes. She's drunk, defenseless, alone. He makes sure no one can see them, and then he begins to stalk her. He lets her see him, lets her get scared. He knows the area. He knows he can take her down easily. He lets her run a little – and then he grabs her."

Nate stared at her with a horrified look. "Damn," he said. "I know you have your way of getting inside their heads and seeing how they think, but… that was chilling."

"Sorry," Laura said, with the ghost of a smile. "But it feels right. This is him. He's living in these places. He must be."

"I agree," Nate nodded. "Which means we just need to figure out where the next spot will be."

"Where was she last seen?"

Laura and Nate looked up at the same time to see a younger detective at the next table over, talking to someone on the phone.

"Okay. And that was last night?" the detective asked. "Right. We're going to have to expedite this, even though it's less than twenty-four hours. Finding her cell phone isn't great news."

The detective put the phone down and Laura got up, stalking over to her table. "What was that phone call about?" she asked, realizing a little too late that maybe her tone was snappier than she had intended.

"There's a missing woman, and we just had her cell phone handed in," the detective said. "Her name is Hayley Sommer. It looks like she's been abducted."

"This sounds like it's one of our cases," Laura said, glancing at Nate. His grim expression seemed to suggest he agreed.

"Well, it wouldn't fit what you were looking for, only…" the detective started, sounding like she was thinking out loud. "She was last seen at a bar late last night, and the witnesses said she was really drunk when she left to walk home. The cell phone thing is new though, right? Your killer normally just kills them right on the spot."

"Where?" Nate asked immediately, grabbing one of his pins from the pot.

The detective came over and leaned over their map, her finger hovering in the air until she found it. "There," she said. She'd pointed to a road along the south edge of the town. Laura leaned in, as did Nate, examining the location.

"There's nothing there," Laura said. "No abandoned structures."

Nate traced a finger along the road, back in the direction of the last victim. "Nothing…" he said, then traced it the other way. "Wait – here. What's this?"

The detective leaned over them to answer his question. "Oh, that's a shelter. It was used by the woodsmen a hundred years or so ago. There's a lot of them around here. With modernization and then the protection of the woodland, they stopped being used. You find them all through the woods. Since the town has expanded, there's even a few like that one that are pretty close to the roads."

Laura looked at Nate, and Nate looked back at her.

"If she's still alive…" she said.

"Do you think she is?" Nate asked. "He killed the others."

"But he had to move her," Laura said. "And even if she's dead – we might catch a trace of him."

"Let's go," Nate said, grabbing the car keys and starting to stride away already.

They had a chance to catch him – and maybe save a life.

Laura ran after him, beating him to the exit.

CHAPTER TWENTY

Laura's eyes were wide and wild as they parked beside the road, the trees right next to them. She stared around in all directions for a clue as to whether he was here – how nearby he was. She couldn't help but feel a fraction of the terror she had absorbed from Joy Kingsley. Here, the woods – it was his domain. This was where he stalked and killed them. And Laura was suddenly all too aware of the things she had in common with the victims, even if there were differences as well.

"Are you ready?" Nate asked. He was looking into the woods with a grim expression on his face. Laura sensed that he felt the heaviness of this place as well.

"I'm not sure I ever will be," Laura said. "But we have to do this. This is what it has all been about, isn't it?"

"What do you mean?" Nate asked.

"The visions," Laura said. She looked back into the trees. Beyond the first few trunks, visibility all but disappeared. The branches were tightly woven enough overhead, the trees evergreen and still leafy at this time of year, that the ground between them was shrouded in darkness even in the early morning light. "They've been leading me here. Telling me that I needed to look into these cases because they aren't finished. There was another victim to come. And now maybe we're too late – but we can still stop him from taking another life, two years from now."

"I hope we're not too late," Nate said, then reached for the doorhandle. "But if we never go in, we will be."

Laura nodded decisively and got out of the car herself. She winced at the sound of the slams as they both closed their doors, wishing it had been quieter. There was no way to tell how deep into the woods their suspect would be. No way to know if he had heard them and already knew they were coming.

Dear God, how she hoped they still had the element of surprise on their hands. Because she had seen how he hunted, and if he had been living here, he would know this area like the back of his hand. They would be sitting ducks.

And yet, what was the alternative? They could have scrambled the whole precinct and brought them down here, and all it might have achieved would be the guaranteed death of the missing young woman. The one he may have in there with him now. Despite the fact that his MO seemed to have been the same in the past – killing them right there and then – he had changed this time. Laura didn't know why, and that terrified her more than anything.

And with even a ten percent chance that the woman might still be alive, they couldn't go in all guns blazing and risk her death as a direct result of police actions.

"We stick together," Nate said, standing beside her on the grassy side of the road, both of them facing the trees as though they were about to go over the edge of the trench into No Man's Land. "If we split up, we'll be targets. We have to stick together, no matter what."

"Agreed," Laura said. Her heart was pounding in her chest. She shouldn't feel this nervous, should she? This was the kind of thing they did all the time. The kind of thing that was just part of their job. Going after a killer wasn't exactly something new.

But she had seen him hunt women as if she was the one being hunted herself, so vivid and clear, and she had felt their fear as if it was her own. Maybe that was the difference, this time.

For the first time, really, she actually felt afraid, as though she was going to die.

"Let's go," Laura whispered, because if she stood there any longer she was going to lose her nerve and get back in the car and drive home to never leave her daughter's side again.

They walked into the trees and within seconds they were in darkness. Laura glanced across at Nate and found she could still make him out – the darkness was not complete – but it was still unnerving. Due to the growth of the trees and other small plants, thick and close together, it was impossible for them to walk directly side by side. They had to diverge around tree trunks, step sideways from time to time. Every time they took a half-step away from one another Laura felt a flare of panic in her chest, prickles of sweat over her body. They had to stick together. That was what they had agreed.

They walked in more or less a straight line from where they had parked, though it immediately became difficult to judge distance. Laura knew that if they kept going straight they would hit the clearing and the relic of the forester's hut, which apparently was the kind of historic landmark you could expect around here. But inside the trees, which might as well have been a different world than the one they had come from, it was difficult to judge distance – and to know if you were even still going the right way or had veered off too far to one side or the other.

When the trees opened up to show them the place they were looking for, it was so sudden that Laura almost gasped. She found herself pulling back, rocking backwards into a spot among the trees, so that they could wait and observe before moving in.

This hut was in better shape than the one they had visited a couple of days ago. It was still mostly intact, and rather than being fully wooden, one of the walls – complete with a half-crumbled chimney – was made of stone. Though the wooden walls were green with slimy moss, it looked like it was actually a pretty decent place to stay if you had no alternative.

And there was smoke coming out of the chimney.

Laura held her breath, looking over at Nate. He nodded; he had seen it too. He made a series of quick gestures with his hands: *I'll go round the front, you go round the back.*

Laura shook her head, breathlessly, fear flaring up inside her.

Nate bit his lip, looked back at the hut, then nodded. He moved both of his hands together this time. *We both go in the front.*

Laura nodded gratefully. She took a breath, then held up three fingers to Nate. They needed to rush in, united, and get this done before the element of surprise wore off – if they had it. She dropped one of her fingers down, then after a beat, another.

She dropped the last finger, and they both charged out of the trees towards the hut.

"FBI! Put your hands in the air!" Laura yelled, hoping this would ward off the possibility of the two of them getting shot by some trigger-happy wild man with a rifle.

"Freeze and put your hands in the air!" Nate shouted alongside her, as they both hit the door. It gave in a shower of splinters, much easier than Laura had expected, and fell to reveal the inside of the cabin.

There was a man there, a man with his hands raised slightly above the level of his shoulders and an expression of pure shock on his face. He was dressed in dirty but warm layers of clothing, his face outlined by a beard, his hair unkempt. He stared at them wildly and wordlessly as if the whole thing had taken his breath away.

Laura took a glance around the rest of the space, looking for the missing woman. The hut was a simple one-room structure with nowhere to hide, and just that quick glance told her immediately that there was no one else here. Whatever he had done with her, she was no longer around. Whether that was a good thing or a bad thing remained to be seen.

That quick glance was all she had time for, taking in the makeshift fire in the stone fireplace and the single broken camping chair that passed as furniture. And on the chair, more telling than anything else, what was clearly a woman's purse. Laura could see the tension in their suspect's body and the way he flinched towards the back of the room – and she knew that they had a runner.

"Stop where you are," she ordered sternly, moving towards him. "Don't move!"

It worked, holding him in place for a moment longer. "What's going on?" he stammered, and his voice was much more timorous than she had expected.

"You're under arrest for murder and attempted murder," Laura said, covering all bases just in case their victim was still alive somewhere. "You have the right -"

She never got the chance to tell him what he had the right to, because in that instant, he turned and ran.

"Hey!" Nate yelled, as he launched himself forward toward the back of the cabin and the other exit, this one in the form of a window that was now boarded with only cardboard. Laura didn't stop to wait for the outcome of that chase. She turned, even as she heard the shredding sound of their man jumping through the window and tearing the cardboard with him, heading for the door they had just come in from. She would try to head their suspect off if he came around the side of the hut.

She almost dislodged a heavy coat hanging off the back of the door as she turned, and her fingers brushing against it gave her a flash headache that she knew had to mean –

She saw the man from the hut, but he was cleaned up, shaved and tidied, wearing a suit. He was nodding and smiling as he shook someone's hand. A flash of a camera went off. Laura caught a glimpse of a banner in the background – something about a program helping vulnerable people get on their feet – an awards ceremony with small, glass trophies being handed out –

Laura ran back out into the open air, stumbling for just a second as she crashed back into reality. Her head barely hurt, and she had enough presence of mind to register the fact that this meant what she had seen was likely a long way off into the future.

She heard a shout and dashed in the direction that it came from, around the side of the hut. As soon as she rounded the corner she saw them: Nate and the man from the hut rolling on the ground, fighting. Nate was the bigger and more muscular of the pair, but the man from the hut was fighting desperately, scratching, and lashing out with his hands and feet in any direction he could, making it hard for Nate to get a grip on him.

Laura wanted to help, but they were going over and over, scrambling madly, and if she had barged in as well it wouldn't have made any positive difference. She couldn't shoot without risk of hitting Nate, and besides, the suspect wasn't armed.

She couldn't shoot. But she could pretend to.

"Stop or I'll shoot!" she shouted, drawing her gun, and pointing it in their direction as if she was actually going to use it.

There was little, if any, reaction from the two men fighting on the cold, hard ground of the wintry woodland. The desperation in their suspect gave him the upper hand for a moment, as he swiped across Nate's face and pushed dirt into his eyes. Nate spluttered and hesitated, enough for the man to get a punch into his gut which left him doubled over. It looked like he was going to lose.

Laura had to take her threat to a level where it would be appreciated.

She pointed her gun upwards and fired it into the air.

The effect was instantaneous. The man on the floor froze, his head swiveling around to this new source of danger, his eyes fixed on her as his body went limp. Nate, still gasping for breath, managed to take advantage of the moment to snap a cuff on one of his wrists. When there was no further struggle, he managed to snap the other cuff into place, properly restraining their suspect.

"Goddamnit," Nate said, panting for breath as he sat up, using his body weight to keep the suspect down.

They had him.

So why did that one flash of a vision Laura had seen make her feel very uneasy indeed?

CHAPTER TWENTY ONE

Laura rested her head in her hands for a moment, trying to catch her breath both physically and mentally. It had been a long morning already, and there were still a few hours to go until the deadline that Rondelle had imposed on them.

A few hours to go, and Nate was already celebrating – but Laura wasn't entirely convinced she felt the same.

"Killer caught," he said, raising a can of soda in the air like it was a beer. Of course, it wasn't going to be a beer until they'd found the last victim, but there was a moment now when everyone felt they could at least celebrate the small win. "Well done."

Laura raised her head and eyed him wearily, blinking slowly. She felt like her head needed to be submerged in a block of ice so it might start to actually function again. She was so tired from everything that had happened, and the repeated visions were a drain.

"Congratulations," someone said, and Laura looked up to see an unfamiliar detective passing by the desk. "They said you caught a serial killer."

She detected both admiration and jealousy in his tone. "Thanks," she said, dully, though she wasn't actually sure she had done what he said.

If they had caught a serial killer, caught him well enough that he was going to go to jail for a very long time, then why had she seen a vision of him cleaning up his act and getting an award in just a few years' time? It wasn't the kind of thing that happened in prisons, and certainly not in the kind of prison he was going to end up in. How could the vision be true?

"You ready for the interview?" Nate asked, tapping her on the arm as though he thought she wasn't paying attention.

"Yeah," Laura said, but she shook her head almost immediately. "No, I'm not. Something's not right."

She was trying to puzzle it all out in her mind. Maybe what she had seen was the possible future before their suspect was caught. Maybe it was what had been awaiting him until he had been arrested. But that didn't make sense, because he was already about to be caught by Nate when she had seen it.

All of which made Laura very nervous, because if their suspect's future involved freedom and turning his life around, then either justice was about to fail…

Or he wasn't their killer after all.

"What's wrong?" Nate frowned.

Laura wanted to tell him what she had seen, but now they had someone who actually seemed like he could have done it in the holding cell; it was like everyone had decided to come into their part of the precinct. It was busy, far too busy for her to guarantee that someone wouldn't overhear what she said.

"We still haven't found the missing victim," Laura said instead. "I don't get it. It doesn't fit his MO. Where is she?"

"Well, hopefully we'll find out as soon as his lawyer gets here and he gets encouraged to talk," Nate said. "He can't keep up the silent act forever. The lawyer will see that it's for the best if he confesses. If he helps us find her and she's still alive, it could sit well with a judge. He's going to see that. After all, he had her purse. We have enough evidence to very strongly imply his guilt."

Laura bit her lip. That still ignored two very real possibilities: first, that she was dead, in which case it wasn't in the killer's interests to give that piece of information at all. And second, that this man was not their killer, in which case all they were doing was wasting time. The man had clearly been afraid when he was confronted by the FBI agents breaking down his door. Laura worried that they were dealing with someone who was too scared to speak in case they ended up getting fitted up for a crime they didn't commit, not someone who was actually guilty. Maybe someone whose only 'crime' had been picking up a dropped purse from the street, thinking he could sell whatever was in it or find some cash.

"The thing is, we don't know what has happened to her at all," Laura said, trying to stress the words in such a way that Nate would realize what she was really trying to say: that she hadn't seen a vision of that death. Surely, with all of these visions flying around, the one that would really be important would be the one that was happening now? Why hadn't she seen it?

And that was the moment when the light bulb went off above her head.

Because she'd had a vision, hadn't she?

That place where they'd found out about the first victim that had set all of this off. The other cabin, the one that was in a much worse state of repair. That was what her vision had shown her. A place she had dismissed because, she believed, she had already seen everything that it had to tell her.

Her visions were never random. Sometimes they didn't make sense until later. Sometimes they turned out to be more trivial than she would have liked. But they were never truly random.

With that being the case, there was only one thing she could do. She had to go there. She had to go back to that first place, opposite Mickey's, and see what was going on. She wasn't going to get any results sitting here and interviewing a man she didn't even fully believe was a killer. She needed to go and follow the lead that her visions were giving her – and trust in them to give her what she needed in the investigation right now.

"Well, we'll find out soon enough," Nate said, nodding up ahead. There was a man in a suit with a briefcase, very clearly a lawyer, making his way across the room.

Laura felt torn for a moment. Her place was here, interviewing their suspect. That was how they always did things. It was what she was expected to do.

But she had to follow this lead, or she was never going to know whether or not she was right. Or worse – she would find out later, and regret it forever.

"I need to go," she said, looking into Nate's face and hoping that he would understand. That he would see she was being driven by something that went beyond protocol or logic. That she would stay if she could, but this thing required her to go out on a limb and take a risk – a risk that might lead to a real result.

"Okay," he said, with a light frown. "Do you need me to come with you?"

Laura thought about it for a brief second, feeling the time pressure of the moment. "No," she said. If she was wrong, someone still needed to stay here and get the interview in the bag. They only had a couple of hours left. If they changed course now in the wrong direction, they would face Rondelle's wrath in an even bigger way than they already did. They had to get a result. It was the only way he wouldn't want to skin them alive. "I'm going to go and check out a location or two where

I think she might be. If I can find her, you don't need his confession. She'll be able to give us a witness statement – or in the worst case, her body will give us answers."

Nate nodded. "Alright," he said, hurriedly getting up from his chair. The lawyer was ready. They needed to start the interview. "I'll have my phone in there. You call me if you find anything or if you need backup – I'll send cars full of cops over to you immediately, got it? Don't rush into anything if you find something suspicious."

"I'll call you," Laura promised. "It's not exactly like this is my first case, Nate. If I'm in over my head, you'll be the first to know I need backup." She wasn't exactly sure how good she was going to be about keeping that promise, but she made it anyway.

Nate nodded once more and rushed off in the direction of the interview rooms, leaving Laura to catch her breath and make her plan.

She scooped up her cell phone and took a photograph of their map, thinking it would come in handy if the clues she found led her elsewhere. She opened Joy Kingsley's file and read it again as quickly as she could, looking in particular for any specifics about how and where the body was found. Everything seemed to tally with what she had seen in her vision. He hadn't moved her, abducted her, taken her somewhere else. She had fallen right where Laura had seen her fall, and that was where he had left her.

So what was so different about this case?

There was only one way she was ever going to find out. Laura took a surreptitious glance around at the other detectives milling around in the bullpen, but she ignored them. None of them had proven themselves to be particularly reliable or trustworthy, having not worked with Laura and Nate during the investigation so far. She didn't want to take along someone she was going to have to babysit and micromanage, and she especially didn't want to have to do it with someone she also needed to lie to. She couldn't tell any of them why she had to go back to this specific place. She couldn't explain her reasoning just then. It was better to go alone.

She walked out of the bullpen and then out of the precinct on her own, trying to tell herself that the way her hands shook when she took the car keys out of her pocket was just because of the adrenaline of the situation.

Out there, somewhere, was a woman who was missing. She was either alive and waiting desperately for help, or she was already dead, and her family deserved to know what had happened to her. Hayley Sommer. Laura didn't know anything about her, but she knew that Hayley was someone's daughter. There were people out there who loved and cared for her. And it was for Hayley that Laura had to do this – and fast.

She got into the car and turned on the ignition before she could lose her nerve, driving out to what she knew could very well be a direct confrontation with a killer.

***

He sat in the old beaten-up chair beside the door, or what was left of it, trying to ignore the chill that leaked through the broken wood. This place wasn't quite as he remembered it. It had seen some hard times since he was last here. But that was okay. It wasn't going to ruin the memory.

He glanced to the side to check on his new girl. Hayley. That was the name that had been printed on the ID he found in her purse. What a lovely name. They always had such lovely names. Joy, Sarina, Alayna – they trickled off the tongue like honey.

Beautiful names for beautiful girls. He never even planned it that way; that was the true beauty of it. He couldn't plan it. The very nature of the way it had to happen meant that planning wasn't possible.

He relied on the place, not the girl. He had to find a place that was right. It had to match up with what he had experienced that very first time, when he was walking home from the bar, an underage drinker who couldn't even get a bus ticket to get him home. That night walking the back roads in the dark, when he had been a teen who felt invincible, who thought nothing of walking such a long distance through the night.

Nothing, until they had found him and set upon him.

There were memories he liked to go over again and again, reliving, and repeating each moment as if it was happening again. And then there were memories he would rather have blocked out forever, which had their way of creeping into his psyche all the same.

He closed his eyes briefly, but that only made the images all the more vivid.

The way they had appeared out of the darkness. He had looked up and seen the sweeping headlights of a car and thought maybe they were going to offer him a ride home when they had stopped in front of him.

He had actually thought, for a moment, that they were there to help him. That was before they had all jumped out from the car, one by one, and started to surround him.

That was before he had looked up into the faces of the men and understood that they weren't there to help him at all.

The men had been bad enough, with their kicking and their trampling, the way they had mocked and insulted him. But the women – the girlfriends of those young men – they had been the worst. He shuddered lightly as he remembered. The way they had pulled down his clothes to humiliate him. The way they had come up with more and more inventive ways to hurt him as the night drew on, highlighting him in the lights of that car, mocking him for the way he cried and whimpered. The way they had exposed him entirely, his soul, left him broken and defeated.

They hadn't killed him. They had come close, but they hadn't killed him. They had left him there on that isolated road, and in the morning he'd been found by someone who took him to hospital and called the police. And he'd said nothing, because he was afraid, and because he didn't want to tell anyone what had really happened.

And he'd spent thirty years telling it over and over again to himself, in the echo chamber of his mind.

Hayley shifted in her sleep, and he redirected his attention to her, telling himself that the past had to stay there. The present, that was what it was about. He was going to make a memory so beautiful that it would overpower the other one, give him something to lovingly trace over and over for the rest of his life. It was taking some patience, but it was going to be worth it. Once she finally woke up and she was ready, it was going to be the best of all of them.

There was something so satisfying about correcting your own mistakes. Joy Kingsley was one of the memories he loved to replay, of course – they were all so cherished – but it had been far from perfect. He had to feed off the terror created by another man. She hadn't been alone, and he hadn't wanted to target her. But when she stepped right into the trees, his trees, in order to get away from someone she perceived as a threat – well, then she had stepped right into the line of his attack. She had seen him. Once she had seen him, he couldn't very well allow her to just go about her business.

Besides, she had been drunk and terrified, and the temptation had been too great.

But she hadn't been his alone. He'd shared her fear with someone else, and that made it a little disconcerting. He wanted the memory to be his and only his. That man had never come forward as a witness, at least to the press, so he didn't even have a name to put to the other figure in his story.

But he could make the story again, and do it properly this time. He could even make it better than the original. That was what he had decided to do.

Hayley stirred again and he smiled to himself, looking down at her. She was going to be perfect for the role. She was just his type: a twenty-something who had been out having far too much fun, dressed in those skimpy clothes like the women who attacked him had worn, those high heels just right for stomping. She wouldn't be using them for that today.

He checked his watch. It was a shame that she had taken so long to wake up. He obviously had underestimated how hard he had choked her. Then again, the alcohol must have played a part as well. She had started breathing again almost right away, but she had stayed asleep. At first he had thought that maybe she was faking, but she'd slept the whole night. Dawn had broken and she was still here.

And that was exciting, too. There would be more cars going by on the road – the illusion that someone might catch them, without really adding any of the danger. That was exciting. He had never done this in the light before. It was going to be so much better for reading the fear on her face, for knowing the look in her eyes when she saw it was over.

He was going to savor this one more than any other.

Hayley opened her eyes, and he shifted to watch her, grinning. It was starting.

"Wha…" she began, looking around blearily. Her voice was a little rough. She cleared her throat and coughed. The next move she made was to try to put her hands to her neck, to find out why it was so sore – but, of course, she couldn't. He had been smarter than that. He had tied her up, so she wouldn't be able to start without him.

"Good morning," he said cheerfully. He waited until her eyes settled on his face, and he grinned wider. He let her see what was behind that grin. What sharp white teeth he had.

Oh, and this was new, and so sweet too. To be able to talk with her. To see how scared she was. To watch that fear grow, to hear it in her voice. So many years he had been doing this, and it was the first time he'd had the chance to really engage.

"Who are you?" she asked, her voice a hoarse whisper, and the fear tingled down all his nerves and thrilled him with its potency.

"I'm your worst nightmare," he said. "But today is your lucky day, because I'm giving you a chance to get away."

"A chance?" she asked, confused. She was still trying to figure out if this was real. If she was really awake, or stuck in a bad dream.

"Get up," he said, bored of her confusion. He wanted her awake and aware. He wanted her to know what was happening to her. She needed to wake up properly.

"What?" she said, groggy still.

"Get up," he snapped, angry now, getting to his feet. He grabbed her by her tied hands and hauled her to her feet. She swayed for a moment but stayed upright, wincing as she found purchase on the floor with her high heels. Stupid girl. She shouldn't wear heels if she couldn't run for her life in them.

"What are you going to do to me?" she asked, and there it was. Beautiful. She understood, now. She knew what her situation was. She must have woken up enough to connect the soreness in her neck with his hands, the ropes around her wrists with his wide and toothy grin.

"I'm going to give you a chance, like I said," he repeated. He nodded over into the corner. "Do you see that?"

She looked, and then she shuddered.

"What is it?" he prompted. He wanted her to play along. It wasn't going to be fun if she didn't play along.

Well, maybe a little.

"It's a gun," she said, barely breathing.

"A rifle," he said triumphantly. "Do you know what that means? It's easy to shoot. You don't have to aim so precisely. So long as you point it at me and pull the trigger, it will throw out these pellets and get a wide range. And they're absolutely lethal, I assure you."

"You want me to shoot you?" she asked. She was trembling. He could feel it where he held her by the hands.

"I want you to have a chance at shooting me," he corrected. "What I really want is to kill you."

She stared at him, almost uncomprehending.

"See, it's like this," he said. "We're going to walk back through the trees a way. You're going to have to remember the route, so keep that in your mind. And when we get back to the starting point, I'm going to cut this rope between your wrists and let you go. With me so far?"

She nodded dumbly, her eyes wide, apparently too frightened even to answer.

"Then you're going to run. And, being the gentleman that I am, I'm going to let you have a head start. Shall we say… five seconds?" he suggested. It wasn't really a question. He didn't pause for her to answer. "Then I'm going to run after you. And you have to win. If you make it back here first and grab that gun and turn around and shoot me, I won't be able to hurt you anymore. Even if you only wing me or graze me, I promise – I won't try to kill you."

"And if I don't?" she croaked, wetting her lips.

"If I catch you before you get the gun, then it's over for you," he said. "I'm going to kill you. I'll stand over you as I watch the life drain from your eyes. That's the game."

"It doesn't sound like much of a game," she whimpered.

"Trust me, I'm going to have fun," he said. He pulled her along after him, tugging at the rope around her wrists to force her to follow. She stumbled one step on her heels before seeming to find her feet again.

They walked through the woods, until he judged they were in about the right place. The sound from the road was still muted enough – and cars passed by infrequently enough – that he figured she wouldn't even realize it was an option in her terrified state. But they were near the place: the place where Joy Kingsley had first seen him.

"Ready?" he asked. He looked into her face, feeding on the raw fear he saw there. She was shaking badly now.

She shook her head, but he grinned and pulled out a viciously sharp pocketknife anyway. He used it to cut through the ropes around her wrists, holding her in place with his hand for just one moment, letting her absorb the knife. Letting her fixate on it.

"On my mark, then," he said. "Three, two, one – go!"

He let go of her hands and she began to run, and he couldn't hold back a chuckle.

He counted to five in his head. At three, she stumbled and caught herself on a tree. At five, she set off running again.

But so did he.

CHAPTER TWENTY TWO

Laura got out of her car at Mickey's and looked both ways, crossing the road rapidly. There was no one around. It was as quiet here as it had been before – a forgotten part of town that most people avoided by taking the highway.

She was at the edge of the trees when she heard a woman scream.

Laura swore and grabbed her gun, holding it ready at her side. She looked ahead into the trees and then hesitated. They were thick here, too. She remembered walking over to the hut the first time, how difficult it had been. How it was tough to know if you were still on the right course. And back then, she hadn't been fully aware she was sharing the woods with a known killer.

Hayley Sommer was alive in there. But where?

She was in the right place. She had come here at the right time. But, frustratingly, she still wasn't sure where to go.

She remembered her promise, and even though every molecule in her body wanted to just charge right ahead, there was still one that she needed to keep her word. She grabbed her cell phone as quickly as she could, almost dropping it with the other hand holding her gun still, and hit speed dial for Nate.

Nothing happened.

She stared at her phone in dismay. There was no service. She bit her lip.

He knew where she was. He knew what she was doing. She had to do something to send him a message, even if she wasn't sure he would get it.

She wrote out the quickest text message she could think of.

SOS

She hit send, shoved the phone back in her pocket where she knew the system would keep trying to send it until it found enough service to do so, and then plunged forward into the trees.

Like every other time she had done it, it was as if she had stepped into a different world. It was quieter here. The sounds of birds, not traffic, dominated the air. And it was darker, the mid-morning sun not penetrating down far enough. She might as well have been here hours earlier, when the dawn was just rising over the horizon, for the amount of visibility she had.

She had to find them. Somewhere in here was Hayley, and somewhere in here was the killer. No matter which one of them she found first, she was going to have to find them.

She flexed her fingers around the handle of the gun, keeping it lowered to the ground as she moved forward cautiously. The last thing she wanted was to be startled by someone bursting out of the trees and then find she had shot Hayley instead of the killer. She needed to proceed with as much caution as possible.

Somewhere up ahead, she heard a rustling noise. A man's voice cried out, then more rustling.

Laura put her thundering heart to one side and ran in the direction of the noise.

Everything was confusion among the trees. Light and shade flashed over her eyes, ruining her vision, and making it hard to understand what she was looking at. The noise of her own passage as she crashed through branches and undergrowth obscured any clues about where the killer and Hayley Sommers might be. All she had to go on was what she had last heard and her own sense of direction – because she was sure the noise had come from the area where the hut was situated.

Laura kept her eyes open, desperately searching for any sign, any glimpse of color, trying to hear any possible noise –

Something hit her arm hard, the arm holding the gun, and she dropped it before she had a chance to react and grip harder. She tripped over something, landing in the dead leaves at the foot of yet another tree, so hard that for a second she was winded. Something grabbed her shoulder. She was dimly aware of her gun spiraling off somewhere – she couldn't see it when she looked to the side. The person grabbing her forcibly turned her over, making her land on her back –

Laura looked up into the face of the killer.

Now that she saw him in person, she recognized him immediately. She had spent so long trying to make other suspects fit the glimpses she'd had of his face, trying to see if their nose was the same or if those same eyes could be the ones that she had seen flashing in the darkness. But now that she saw him again, she knew that had been foolish. The man in front of her now – none of them looked anything like him at all.

His face was cold, hard, closed. He looked empty. Dead inside already. Like there was absolutely nothing she could say or do, no sob story, no plea for clemency that would ever get through. His mind was made up. She was going to die.

And then he frowned at her in total confusion, like he had no idea who he was looking at – and Laura realized he must have thought she was Hayley.

And in that same instant, she realized she had a moment of advantage – and she took it, pushing him hard in the chest and using the same momentum to roll up and to the side, getting to her feet. She spun around to face him, ready to fight tooth and nail if need be –

And was confronted only with the sight of his back retreating from her.

Laura caught her breath, starting to run after him and then stopping. Her gun. She needed her gun. If she had that she could have just shot him now, but – where was it?

She dropped to her knees again hastily, searching the ground, pushing aside brush and fern growth, trying to find it. She couldn't even get a glimpse. Laura despaired, realizing she was unarmed now and there was nothing she could do about it – not in enough time to make a difference. There would probably need to be a search effort from the local precinct in order to help her track it down in a place like this, where it could have spun off in any direction and gone under anything.

But Hayley – Hayley needed her now.

Laura got back to her feet, looking in the direction the killer had gone and trying to listen. If he came upon her again, she wasn't sure the fact that he was surprised to see her would make enough of a difference. In all likelihood, he was just going to turn around once he had killed Hayley and come back to take care of her as a witness.

She couldn't fight him – not well, at least. He was bigger. Heavier. Used to killing women with his bare hands – at least five of them. Hayley would make six if he managed it. And Laura wasn't even sure whether her message to Nate had gone through, let alone how long it would take him to get here if it had.

But still. She had a duty.

The hut – she had seen that in her vision. Not the woods. Not Mickey's or the roadside. The hut.

She had to trust in her vision.

Hoping she still had her bearings, Laura set off in the direction of the hut at a run, believing – because she had to – that she would find Hayley there.

She ran full out until she burst into the clearing, experiencing just one moment of pure exhilaration at the fact that she had been right – she had kept her sense of direction even in the depth of the woods. It was swiftly followed by fear.

Out here, she was vulnerable. A sitting duck. He would be able to see her from the tree line easily.

And it occurred to her there was a possibility that the reason she couldn't find her gun was because he had taken it with him.

Laura swallowed hard and rushed forward, seeking the relative safety of the hut. She grabbed the door and rushed inside –

And had to bite back a scream.

The other woman, the one holding a rifle and pointing it right at her, also visibly restrained herself, her face a mask of shock. There was a moment when the two of them held their breath, Laura because she didn't want to be shot and the woman, who had to be Hayley, presumably because she was getting over the fact she had almost shot someone.

"Who are you?" she whispered, a stage whisper, gesturing with the gun for Laura to go deeper inside the room and away from the door.

"I'm an FBI agent," Laura whispered back, following the directions. They both turned and looked towards the half-constructed door. The only vantage point from which they would be able to see the killer coming. "You're Hayley Sommer?"

"Yes!" Hayley said, and almost sagged in relief. "You came to find me?"

Laura nodded. "I'm sorry. He managed to disarm me. I don't know if he has my gun or if it's just gone."

Hayley stared at her. "Wait. You're on your own?"

Laura nodded, guilty, feeling the fact that she had let her down in her bones. If she had managed to neutralize the killer out there in the woods, she could have been a hero. Instead, she was the idiot agent who got herself captured as well by showing up alone and unprepared.

There was a noise outside, and Hayley swore, lifting the gun and pointing it squarely at the door again.

"I should take that," Laura said. "I have firearms training."

"No way," Hayley said, with a short, humorous laugh. "No offense, but this is my only defense. I'm not handing it over to someone else. For all I know, you're part of this."

"I'm not," Laura promised, but she could also see how hard it would be to believe that. "Do you know how to fire it?"

"Just point and shoot, right?" Hayley asked, setting the rifle to her eye again and keeping it trained on the door.

"Watch out for rebound, and take the extra millisecond to re-aim when he appears," Laura advised. If she wasn't going to be able to do it herself, all she could manage would be to give her as many tips as possible.

"I've got it," Hayley said, and there was so much determination in her voice that Laura actually believed her.

There was a sound outside – a sound that had both of them tensing up.

Laura didn't know what to do with herself. She was unarmed. If the killer had a gun, she had no way to defend herself – nothing to use as a shield in here, nowhere to hide. If he was unarmed and Hayley missed her shot, he was still strong and powerful – enough to win in a direct one-on-one fight. The fact there were two of them now was the thing they had going for themselves. But even in that advantage, Hayley was the one with the weapon. Laura just had to stand by and wait.

She hated it.

The noise from outside came again, and this time it was more obvious: a footstep.

What was he going to do? Try to creep up on them? Laura looked at Hayley and saw that she was shaking, the point of the gun trembling in the air.

"Are you in there?" the killer called out, in a singsong voice. Laura felt the hairs on the back of her neck stand up. "Did you get my present?"

"What is he talking about?" Laura muttered quietly enough she hoped only Hayley would hear her.

"The gun," Hayley murmured back. "He left the gun here to make it more exciting or whatever."

Something jumped at the pit of Laura's stomach. That wasn't right. Why would he leave the means for them to kill him? Why would he make it possible for Hayley to get away, when all the others had no chance at all?

Why change his MO this drastically?

Unless…

The door burst open in a shower of splinters and flying moss, and there he was – standing there – grinning at the two of them. Hayley aimed the gun and pulled the trigger, and –

And nothing happened.

Only an empty click that had Laura looking around at her in despair.

"Oh, come on," he said, his eyes sparking with a kind of manic glee. "You didn't think I would really leave it loaded, did you?"

CHAPTER TWENTY THREE

Laura's shock gave way to something else. Not fear, not determination, not courage. Just pure bare fight or flight instinct, no logic or reason, no thought process. All she knew was that there were two of them and one of him, and he was a threat, and he needed to go.

She lunged forward before Hayley could recover. The man's hands were empty. No gun, at least not one that he was carrying in plain sight. She wasn't going to give him the time to reach into his pockets. Laura collided with him in the air, so hard that he stumbled backwards and then fell, tripping over the step leading into the hut.

He landed on his back, the air knocked out of him. Laura struggled to get on top of him, sitting up so she could lean back and land a punch right into his face, but he recovered too quickly. He grabbed her hips and threw his own weight to the side, throwing her onto the ground. He was fast and strong. Laura kicked out and connected with his shin, not the softer target she was aiming for, and rolled away as fast as she could.

He was there when she came up again, right behind her. She aimed a punch at his stomach this time, trying to wind him again and get him to double over, but he simply twisted aside and then slammed his hand into the middle of her arm as it passed him. It was knocked down against the earth and then he was pinning her other arm, using sheer force to stop her from swinging that one at him as well, keeping her down. Laura tried to sit up, to push against him, but it was useless. He had her pinned against the earth, unable to move, unable to stop him.

Something hit his head so hard she heard a noise, and then it was Hayley standing over her instead of the killer, clutching the rifle butt-first in her hand.

She reached down, offering a hand to Laura to help her get to her feet. Laura took it, got up, and spun around – but too slow. The killer was already back on his feet as well, tapping his palm against his head and bringing it away with a light coat of blood, then snarling at the two of them.

He wasn't playing anymore. He was angry. And he clearly knew exactly who he wanted to take it out on.

Laura stepped forward, wanting to keep Hayley behind her for protection, and he must have interpreted it as an aggressive move. He rushed Laura, then Hayley, using his body weight and momentum to knock both of them down. Hayley tried to get up and grappled with him briefly before he threw her to the ground. Her head rebounded, and Laura was grateful that they were lying on soft soil instead of rocky terrain.

She swung her legs to tangle with his, tripping him and making him crash to the ground between them. He lunged for Hayley's gun but she pulled it out of reach and then thrust it back, connecting with his chest. He cried out and grabbed the rifle as she tried to take it back again, and she tugged helplessly a couple of times, unable to shift it. He couldn't get the weapon. It was the only advantage they had. Laura threw herself on him, hands extended, and deliberately began to scratch viciously at his face and neck from behind.

With a yowl, the killer let go of the gun and reached up to stop Laura's hands instead. Laura didn't see what happened next – too busy trying to wrench her hands out of his grasp without allowing him to crush or break her fingers. But there was a sickening crunch and then a groan, and he let go of her hands.

Laura scrambled to her feet and a ready stance, then looked down.

His eyes were closed, his face pale. There was another fresh red mark on the other side of his head, neatly opposite the one that had broken the skin before. Hayley was panting beside her, still holding the rifle at the ready, butt-first like a bludgeon.

"Is he dead?" she gasped.

Laura knelt, cautious, always watching for signs that he would wake up and attack again or that he was faking. She found his neck with two fingers, sought out his pulse.

"No, he's just unconscious," she said.

"Should we kill him?" Hayley asked.

Laura glanced up to give her a wry look. "I have a better solution," she said. She pulled a pair of handcuffs out of the pocket of her windbreaker and grabbed the killer's hands one by one, cuffing them behind his back as she rolled him.

There was a moment of silence, the two women still breathing heavily. It was like the whole of the woods around them had gone quiet. Then they both heard it at the same time: the sound of something crashing through the trees.

They shared a glance of alarm.

Was the killer not working alone? Was there someone else out there ready to come and avenge him?

"Laura!" a voice shouted wildly, and Laura's eyes slid closed for a second in relief.

"Nate!" she shouted back. "We're over here!"

There was the sound of even more frantic progress through the trees and then Nate burst out into the clearing in front of them, his face full of clear panic. "Jesus! What's happening?"

"It's him," Laura said, indicating the man lying on the ground at his feet. "It's him. And this is Hayley Sommers."

Nate paused right in front of them, staring. He was giving her a funny kind of look. The kind of look that said *I can't believe you did this again – but thank God you're okay.*

"Is anyone hurt?" he asked, glancing between all three of them. Hayley and Laura were catching their breath now. Hayley was leaning on the rifle like it was a walking stick.

"We're a little bruised and battered," Laura said. "He's got a couple of head injuries."

"Anything that needs medical attention?" he asked, putting the question directly to Hayley.

She shook her head, swallowed, then shrugged. "I was out cold all night," she said. "I don't know what he did to me. My throat hurts."

Laura could see bruises in the shape of fingers on her neck. "She should get checked out," she said.

There was a beat, and then Hayley burst into tears. The adrenaline was leaving, now. The shock was right behind it. Laura put a reassuring hand on her back, turning to Nate. There were police officers emerging from the trees around him now, all of them clearly on high alert, decked out in bulletproof gear and making their way through the undergrowth awkwardly.

"We need to get her under a foil blanket, too," Laura said. "She's been out here all night."

Nate nodded and turned to start barking orders at the locals. Within short order, the killer had been assessed and hauled up so they could carry him back to their transport, Hayley was being led through the trees by an EMT, and Laura – blessedly – was holding a takeout cup of coffee.

"You ready to go?" Nate asked her.

Laura glanced back at the hut – the one she had seen in her vision, the thing that had led her here in the first place. The full circle moment.

"Can't I just stay here so we don't have to face Rondelle?" she whined, and Nate only laughed.

CHAPTER TWENTY FOUR

Laura took a deep breath.

"Are you sure you're ready for this?" Nate muttered.

"Agents Lavoie and Frost, don't just stand around out there," Division Chief Rondelle barked from inside his office. There was no way he could see them – the door was closed. Laura thought incredulously that he must have somehow managed to hear Nate's low voice from through the thick wood.

Laura gave Nate a helpless shrug – *it doesn't matter if I'm ready or not* – and pushed the door open.

"Sir," she said immediately, heading over to stand in front of his desk. They always seemed to stand in this room. They were there for a briefing or to be shouted at, and nothing else.

"Report," Rondelle said immediately.

Nate and Laura exchanged another look. "We were able to identify the location the killer had taken his would-be last victim through analysis of his previous crimes," Laura said. "We got there in time to save her and bring him into custody alive."

"I know about that part," Rondelle said, staring both of them dead-on. "I have that report on my desk. What I want to hear about is why you were there in the first place."

"Sir?" Laura asked. "We noticed the old cold cases were all similar and saw they must have been connected."

"And how did you know to look at those cases in the first place?" Rondelle asked. When there wasn't an immediate answer, he continued. "I have another report on my desk here saying that the case files weren't accessed recently until one Dean Marsters from the tech department opened the first one. And lo and behold, in his call logs I found a call from your personal cell number, Agent Frost. Right before he looked up the case. So, do you want to tell me why Dean Marsters was looking up cases for you if you didn't even know about them until that point?"

Laura started to open her mouth, trying to think on the spot – but apparently, Rondelle wasn't yet done.

"I know you didn't know anything about any of the cases until then because neither of you have ever accessed the files," he said. "Nor has anyone else in this entire office. In fact, nor has anyone in any police system for at least a year. So, what I'm wondering is, how did you even know to ask Dean to look them up for you?"

"We had an anonymous tip-off," Nate said. "At first, we weren't sure it was even legitimate. That's why we didn't say anything at first. But when we checked out the location and discovered that it had been the site of a previous murder, we started to take it seriously. We just didn't have any evidence – it was all gut instinct."

"And you couldn't have told me this when I called you? Or after you realized the cases were connected?" Rondelle demanded.

"We thought you would be mad that we were chasing a hunch," Laura said, risking an ad-lib. "Actually, Agent Lavoie thought we should come back to HQ and leave the case alone. It was me who insisted. I just had that feeling – and my gut is never wrong. I didn't want to take the risk that the tip-off was right and there was an active killer in the region."

There was a little sadness in having to claim that someone told them what to look for. After all, it erased the skill it had taken on their part to actually put the pieces together. Still, it was better than being quizzed on the truth.

Rondelle looked both of them over carefully for a long moment. Laura thought he was going to accuse them of lying. She almost opened her mouth to say something, anything, to throw herself on the sword so at least Nate's job would be safe.

Then Rondelle sighed and shook his head. "Next time, you come to me from the beginning," he said. "I don't care what you think or believe will happen. You tell me. If I find out you've been investigating on your own again, I'll suspend you and you can do it on your own dime. Got it?"

"Yes, sir," Nate and Laura both muttered at the same time.

There was a pause. Rondelle shook his head again. "I know you two have some… way of doing things. Some secret. I'm not stupid. I did my time as an agent, remember. But, frankly, so long as you keep getting results, I don't care. Don't tell me. Keep doing whatever you do. Just… remember that you answer to me."

Laura and Nate nodded quietly, both of them keeping their heads bowed so as to show their respect.

"I was an agent myself, remember," he went on. "I know the temptation to get your information from less than clean sources, just to make sure you get it. If you feel you can't tell me where you get your informants from, then it may be best to reassess who you work with. If I find out you're backroom dealing, you're gone, or worse, you're going to prison. Do I make myself clear?"

"Yes, sir," Laura said, her voice quiet. Nate murmured the same. Rondelle was way off the mark, but it didn't matter. So long as they kept him thinking they were dancing along the line, and that was why they didn't want to say anything, he wouldn't press them further. It was better this way.

"Alright," he sighed. "Dismissed."

It wasn't the praise they might have hoped for after solving the case – but it would do.

***

Laura settled down at the kitchen counter, feeling like she was just getting off a rollercoaster ride. There was something in the ritual of coming over to Chris's place after a case was finished. Coming over for coffee and conversation, a debrief into the real world again, a chance to remember she was more than just an agent and that the world contained more than just evil.

Chris set the steaming cup of coffee down in front of her and Laura inhaled the bitter scent, feeling herself coming back to normal.

"So, you didn't get yourself stabbed, shot, burned, or knocked unconscious on this one?" he asked, like he needed to double-check.

"No," Laura confirmed with a smile. "I got off totally scot-free."

"I'm impressed," Chris said.

"Well," Laura said, picking up her cup and taking a sip. "At least, I only got a few bruises."

Chris shook his head in exasperation, making her laugh. "So, did you figure out what that whole danger thing was about?"

He said it casually, but Laura sensed he was nervous. He wanted her reassurance. She smiled into her coffee cup, hoping that would put him at ease. "Not yet. But I haven't seen anything darker, either."

"That's good," Chris nodded. "Right?"

"It's certainly not bad," Laura said. "We just have to be patient and wait for a vision to come up."

"About that," Chris said thoughtfully. "I was wondering if you'd let me run some tests. I have a buddy at the hospital who said he'd let me use the MRI machine without it being logged. What do you think?"

Laura stared back at him for a minute. In her head, all she could hear was Nate's warning before she had told Chris the truth about her ability. He'd been afraid for her back then. He'd suggested that she didn't know Chris well enough to know how he would react. He'd said that Chris would want to experiment on her. To test her. To see her as a medical phenomenon that he could present for clout, ruining her life in the process.

"Why?" she asked, blurting the word out almost in panic.

"Well, I know you don't know how to control the visions well, and it bothers you," Chris said. "I was thinking, if I can see how your brain is firing – maybe even get it to track what happens during a vision – you might be able to understand it more. Maybe figure out what the link is so that you can trigger them on your own."

"You want to help me have visions easier?" Laura asked.

"Okay, I admit, my motives aren't entirely altruistic," Chris said with a slight blush. "I, ah. I would feel a lot better if you were able to check on Lacey and Amy from time to time. Deliberately, you know. Check that there wasn't anything bad in their future."

"Oh," Laura said, considering it. "I guess that would be nice to have."

"And you could save more lives, of course," Chris added hastily. "It's not just about what I would gain personally. I know how important your job is to you. If you can master your abilities more, you'll be able to help people more. Right? If you could get visions to appear whenever you wanted, you'd be able to catch killers more easily."

"That's true," Laura said. She nodded slowly, considering it. "I think it might be a good idea."

"Alright, then," Chris said with a grin. He reached out, entwining their fingers together over the top of the kitchen counter. "And, um. There was something else as well."

"Yeah?" Laura asked, taking another gulp of her coffee.

"It's nice when you get to come back from a case and come over here, right?" he asked. "You know – coffee in the kitchen, waiting for the girls to finish school. All of that."

"Yes, I do enjoy it," Laura said, wondering where this was going.

"Well, it's a shame that you can't do it while I'm working," he said, looking deep into his own coffee cup. "Come over here, I mean."

"I just wait for you," Laura said.

"Right," Chris said, still seeming as if he was trying to convince his coffee of something. "Right, but, I mean – what if you didn't need to wait?"

"Because I had a key?" Laura asked, thinking she might have discovered what he was offering.

"No," Chris said, then made a face. "Well, yes. What I mean is – what if you lived here?"

Laura blinked at him. "You want me to move in?"

Chris groaned. "It's too soon, isn't it? I knew it was too soon. I just – I got overexcited. I want to be with you all the time, and I know you're not ready for that, I just…"

"Chris," Laura interrupted, making him look up at her when she took his hand. "Chris, I'd love to move in with you."

And that would have been an incredibly happy moment, if it wasn't for the headache snapping at her temple and dragging her towards –

Everything was gray and swirling, like she was completely entrenched in the gray fog she'd seen from Chris and Nate. This time, though, it was like she was trying to see a vision through it.

Darkness was swirling at the edge of her vision, like it used to when she was too close to Zach. Like something was messing with her abilities. But this…

She couldn't put her finger on it, but it was like she was having a vision of a vision. Seeing things in the future going dark again.

But Zach wasn't around anymore. So, what –

Laura blinked, back in the room with Chris.

"Did you see something?" he asked, his voice tense again. "Something to do with moving in?"

"No," Laura said, and frowned. "No, not that. I think… I think I have to give a friend of mine a visit soon. Something's up and I don't know what. Actually, maybe I should give him a call."

"Go, go," Chris said, and then grinned. "It'll give me a chance to get the champagne out and a couple of glasses.

Laura smiled at him. "You do that. I'll be back as soon as I've spoken to him."

She walked away, down the hall, putting the cell phone to her ear as she went. She dialed Zach's number and waited, holding her breath.

She needed to know if he was alright. There was a tight feeling in her gut she didn't like, a breathlessness in her chest.

The phone rang to voicemail, a stern robotic voice telling her to leave a message. Laura wet her lips. "Zach," she said into the machine. "I really hope you're just busy right now and haven't seen your phone ringing. Just… just let me know if you get this, okay? Call me back. It's Laura."

She ended the call and tapped the phone against her chin. She felt worse, now. Like there was something awful about to happen. The Titanic going down or a tsunami or that boat that had sunk off South Korea with all the schoolkids inside.

Maybe it wasn't water-related at all, but she still had a very bad feeling.

"Chris," she called out, hearing how even her own voice sounded strange now. "Maybe hold that champagne. I think I have to go see him. Something's not right."

Chris appeared in the doorway to the kitchen, holding a chilled bottle of champagne and a slightly crestfallen look. The bottle wasn't open, though. Laura had called out to him in time. "Do you need me to come with you?"

Laura thought about it. She had a reputation for rushing into things on her own and getting into trouble, she knew. Nate was always on her back about it, and now Chris was, too. But if she took along someone who didn't have the same powers that she did, or even the basic ability to defend themselves, then she could be leading them into danger.

And someone needed to be here for the girls.

"No," Laura said. "No, I'm sure it's nothing. I'll just go and come right back. Hey, why don't we have dinner tonight – you, me, and Amy? Somewhere nice?"

"Sounds like a great idea," Chris said, brightening slightly. "I'll make the reservation."

"I'll be home soon," Laura said, and the grin he gave her as she turned to leave was enough to lighten the whole rest of her day.

If only she actually believed what she'd said, that Zach wasn't in any trouble at all. Because she had a nervous feeling she was about to walk into the most danger of her life.

CHAPTER TWENTY FIVE

The psychic leaned forward on his hand, admiring the fear in the old man's face.

"You know what the best part of hunting down psychics is?" he asked. "It's the fact that none of them know it's coming. It's hilarious, isn't it? The one thing that could save your life would be having your own vision of your death – but because I'm here, you can't see anything at all."

"I saw it," the old man said. Zach, his name was. He was behaving very calmly, but it was nonsense. The psychic could see the fear on his face. He was just trying to buy time, trying to figure out a way to get out of the ropes tying him to the chair. "I didn't know how it would happen, but I knew I was going to die. I've been feeling it for a long time."

"Oh?" the psychic said, barely interested but playing along. As much as he loved killing other psychics and draining their powers, it was sometimes useful to listen to them for a little while first, too. They could tell him things he wasn't going to learn any other way. Sometimes one of them even knew a trick, or a technique, that he didn't know. That was another of the ways in which he had managed to continue to become the strongest of them all: to steal their knowledge first before their power.

"It's funny," the old man said, and the psychic just barely held back from rolling his eyes. "I thought it was all over when I had a heart attack. They resuscitated me from that, and I suppose I thought that was it – I'd beaten death. But of course, then I had that same feeling again afterwards, and I knew. My time is up. It wasn't the heart attack I was waiting for. It was you."

"And here I am," the psychic said, spreading his arms wide dramatically. So much for learning anything useful. If all psychics got a vague premonition about their own deaths beforehand, it was something he would learn by himself sooner or later. And since he'd never experienced anything like that, he figured he wasn't going to die any time soon. "Well, enough talking. I think it's time we get down to business."

"Why are you doing this?" Zach asked, interrupting him just as he was getting up. "You must be a psychic like I am. That's why my powers aren't working. So, why are you doing it?"

He smiled slightly to himself. "You don't know, do you?" he asked. "When one psychic kills another, the survivor gets to take their power. I'm stronger than I've ever been – stronger than anyone who ever existed."

"Why?" Zach asked.

The psychic stopped, staring at him. Was he serious with that question? Why?

"To be the strongest," he said, as if that answered everything – because it did.

"Aren't you going to give me some terribly sad backstory?" Zach asked. "Aren't you going to tell me how your mother died when you were young and you just wished you could have saved her? Or perhaps it's fear – fear of something bad happening to yourself – and you want to learn how to see the whole of your own future by getting stronger?"

"No backstory," the psychic said idly. "No tragedy. I just want to be the strongest. And as long as people like you are around, there's always the chance that one of you will kill me to get stronger instead."

"But why would anyone else do that?" Zach asked. He sounded nonplussed. "I don't want to be the strongest. I have no ambitions. Especially not if I would have to kill people to gain that strength."

"Enough of this," the psychic snarled. The stupid old man was just trying to save his own life. If he had the opportunity, he would be a killer like the psychic. "I'm done talking. It's time that you gave me your power." He picked up the knife he had set down next to himself when he had first tied Zach up, walking closer to him. He grabbed Zach by the hair.

Zach lifted his eyes almost in defiance. The old man's neck was open. Ready for a slash that would drain his life and give his power an outlet. "You don't have to do this to get stronger," he said.

"Stupid old man," the psychic said. "I'm not going to believe anything you say. You were lying. You never saw any of this coming."

"But I did," someone said.

The psychic was aware of a breeze at his neck, the passage of someone moving behind him. His eyes darted to the side and he spun, ready to use the knife – only to falter when he saw that she was holding a gun.

The curtain in the window behind her shifted a little with the wind outside. He'd left it open. How clumsy of him. He hadn't imagined that anyone would be coming to save him, not out here.

She must have climbed in while his back was turned.

She was supposed to find out at the funeral. He was supposed to attack her there. This wasn't right.

"You," he said, with some surprise. It was a change in the order of proceedings, yes. He was supposed to kill Zach first and then get her at the funeral. But the funny thing about causing a vision blind spot was that it affected him as well – but she, this agent, must have been outside of it. She must have seen what was going to happen after all.

It didn't matter. It was just a change in the order. He would kill her first, then her friend. The old man was tied up. He wasn't going anywhere.

"Put down the knife," she said. The gun was pointing right at him.

But she was law enforcement. She had rules to follow. She had to think before she shot.

"No," he said, smiling pleasantly. "Why don't you put down the gun?"

"Zach's right," the agent said. "You don't have to do this. Psychics don't get stronger by killing one another. It's proximity. If you spend time near another psychic, you get stronger when you leave them again."

"It's true," Zach nodded. "I started being able to do all kinds of new things since I met Laura. Kinds of visions I'd never had before."

"And I've started having stronger, more visceral visions since I met Zach," Laura explained.

"Strong enough that you could see me coming," the psychic murdered. That was something to watch out for. Whatever incremental gains they would have from being around each other, even if it wasn't as strong as his gains from murder, they were getting stronger. He had to find a way to stop them from getting together in the future. It was the only way to guarantee his own survival.

"See?" The agent tried to plead. "This is madness. Just stop. You don't have to kill anyone. You can get stronger by being around us."

He looked up at her. Through all the fog, the uncertainty, the fear that they would turn on him, one thing became so vividly clear to him that its existence could not be denied. It was as strong as if he had seen it in a vision.

"Even if I agreed to stop," he said. "You're an FBI agent. You can't let me go free. And you can't risk that I'll tell the world about psychics and out you. You have to kill me."

Laura bit her lip. "And because you believe that you'll never stop killing."

"Yes." He looked at her, and he knew. There was only a split-second to see it, but he knew. He had misjudged her. She wasn't bound by the rules at all. He lunged forward with the knife, seeing his last opportunity to stop her from taking him out.

Then she fired, and he knew more than felt that the bullet entered his heart, and the last thing he thought was to wonder why he was suddenly looking up at the ceiling.

***

"I'm sorry he came for you," Laura said, shaking her head.

Zach blinked, looking away from the lukewarm cup of thin coffee the local precinct had been able to provide for him. The fact that they were sitting in a private waiting area and not an interview room was a blessing, but Laura still wished they had allowed Zach to go home.

Or, at least, to leave. His home wasn't a pleasant place to be right now, with that bloodstain soaked into the carpet.

"It's not your fault," Zach said. "You didn't force him to become a killer. He decided that all on his own."

"I should have seen it sooner," Laura said. "He was the danger I sensed. The danger all around me. I should have figured out that someone was after me – and that they would target my friends to do it. I saw his intentions in my vision. He was going to kill you to lure me out on my own, make me vulnerable."

Zach shook his head. "It's still not your fault. You're not responsible for the actions of others, whether you see them or not."

Laura sighed and nodded. "I guess. That's one of my faults, I suppose. Always trying to take responsibility for everything."

"It is," Zach said seriously. "You should stop."

Laura took a sip of her own coffee and winced, setting it aside. It wasn't even worth it for the hydration. "You're right." She smiled. "Well, now we've figured out this thing about getting stronger with proximity, maybe we can hang out a bit more between cases. You can help me stay on the straight and narrow."

Zach chuckled. "If you'll have time. Don't you have your daughter and that handsome boyfriend of yours keeping you busy?"

"I do," Laura smiled. "Actually, I have some news on that front. We've decided to move in together."

Zach's eyes widened with joy. He had the kind of expression on his face that Laura always imagined a father would share with their daughter at that kind of news. Her own father had died long before her first marriage, before Lacey, before all of it. Seeing it on Zach's face felt like one more piece of the puzzle that was her life was finally clicking into place. "Laura, that's fantastic news! Oh, I know you'll be very happy together. And after that? What do you think? Is marriage in the cards?"

Laura blushed a little, looking away with a grin. "I don't know. I suppose we'll see how it goes first."

"If you do, you have to let me come," Zach said, a twinkle in his blue eyes. "I know you won't want me to mess up any visions you might have in case something goes wrong on the day, but I'll sneak in at the last minute."

"I will," Laura said, then laughed and shook her head, flustered. "If it ever comes to that!"

Zach laughed merrily. "Well, I'm glad things are going well for you, anyway. I'm sure catching yet another serial killer will be another feather in your cap, too."

Laura bit her lip nervously. She hadn't yet fully allowed herself to consider the ramifications of this. Was Rondelle going to be glad that she had stopped a killer – or mad because he'd just told her to stop investigating things alone?

Of course, it hadn't happened like that. That was her defense. She could tell them that Zach had picked up the phone, not his voicemail, and that he'd said something very quickly that made her realize he was in danger. It would match up with the phone records. It would be an easy lie to sell.

And if Rondelle didn't buy it…

Well, Laura wasn't worried about that anymore. She had a loving partner, access to her daughter again, and a good enough relationship with Nate that she really did believe that psychic detective agency was a backup option they could take. She had been sober for long enough now to believe she had a strong chance of not falling off the wagon again, and her powers were stronger than ever – and she understood how to use them more than she ever had.

She had friends around her, a happy home life, and she was good at her job. Good enough to follow it in a different direction if she needed to. She had no reason to be afraid anymore.

"I guess it is," she said, because she could put feathers in her own cap without waiting for approval from her boss.

Her cell phone started to ring in her pocket, and Laura grabbed it with a quick apology. She glanced at the screen and saw Nate's name. Was he calling about a case? Or did Rondelle already want to talk to her about all of this?

She stepped out into the hall and answered it, pressing it to her ear. "Hi, Nate."

"Laura!" he said. "I was just wondering – do you have Lacey this weekend?"

"I do," Laura said, wondering where this was going.

"Great!" Nate said. "Oh, and is Chris working?"

"No, he has the weekend off usually," Laura said.

"Okay, great," Nate said. "Well, I was wondering if you all wanted to come over and hang out. It's supposed to be the first sunny weekend of the year. I was thinking of doing a barbecue. What do you think? Amy's welcome as well, of course."

"That sounds great," Laura grinned. "What's brought this on?"

"I thought it was about time we hang out properly," Nate said. "You know, like partners."

Laura laughed. "That's a great idea," she said, glancing back at Zach through the window in the door. "I've got a lot to tell you, actually."

"I can't wait," Nate said.

Laura thought about her life, about how different it was now to how she had been even a year ago. About how happiness seemed to be attacking her from all sides, determined not to let her go.

"Me either," she said, her voice choked with emotion.

***

Laura shook her head and laughed.

"No, seriously," Nate said. "She won't be stopped."

“I can imagine,” Chris said. He rubbed his forehead with the hand that held the beer bottle. “Oh, man. I shouldn’t have come to this barbecue. Now you’re going to have me even more worried about her every time she goes on a case.”

“How do you think I feel?” Nate asked. “I’m supposed to be there in the field with her, and somehow she always manages to get herself into danger without me. Like, I’m *right there*. Use me!”

“Be careful what you wish for,” Laura said, pretending to be more disgruntled than she actually felt. “I’ll put you in the path of danger next time, instead.”

“It might be better if no one was in the path of danger,” Zach suggested mildly. He’d tagged along after they’d realized they had nothing to fear from being together now, given that Laura and Nate were likely to be on rest from cases for at least a week or two until Rondelle properly forgave them. “Just a thought.”

“Yeah, I’m with Zach on this one,” Chis agreed. He took a sip of his beer. “I’d better go check on the girls.”

“I can see them,” Laura said, tilting her head slightly. Amy and Lacey were playing on the floor in Nate’s living room, surrounded as always by what seemed like an improbable number of dolls. “They’re fine.”

“Good, because you two don’t want to go anywhere right now,” Nate announced, clicking a pair of tongs together in mid-air. “Meat’s up.”

“Great!” Laura said, and the others all murmured their appreciation as well, moving to grab paper plates and form a loose line while Nate dished out burgers and sausages.

“This is amazing,” Chris said, taking his first bite. “Nate, where did you get this grill? This looks like the kind of thing that would go nicely in my backyard.”

“Our backyard,” Laura corrected him with humor dancing in her eyes. “And when do you have time to grill between your shifts and the girls?”

“I’d grill *for* the girls,” Chris said. “Actually, I better go call them for some food or they’ll be mad they missed out.”

“Look, you don’t need to argue,” Nate chuckled. “Just come round here anytime you want. A man doesn’t buy a grill this big and then only use it to cook for himself.”

"We should make this a regular thing," Laura nodded. "Maybe it can be our ritual."

"Ritual?" Nate cocked his head.

"Yeah," Laura nodded. "I'm always hearing other agents talking about their rituals for when they finish a case."

"I've seen that on TV," Zach added helpfully.

"We should come over like this any time we finish a case," Laura said. "It's perfect. It's a good time for me to see Zach, because I won't need my powers functioning fully for a little bit. And if we find any other psychics out there, we can hang out together, too. And who doesn't love food as a way to celebrate?"

"Alright," Nate said seriously, nodding. "Let's do that."

Chris re-emerged from the house with the girls, balancing his plate in one hand and keeping an eye on them as they ran around his legs to get to the food. They chattered and laughed as Nate held out food to them in his shiny tongs, first holding up a finger to caution them that it was hot.

"Don't run near the grill, girls," Laura said, resting a hand on Lacey's head for a moment to muss her hair. "You can take your food back inside to your dolls if you want."

The girls screamed with glee, which seemed to be their main method of communication lately, and then ran back inside with their plates full.

Laura sat down in a lawn chair beside Chris and sighed contentedly. She looked around the small backyard. Her partner. Her live-in boyfriend. Her psychic mentor and friend. Her daughter, and the one she was moving towards adopting. All the people who mattered to her were within a ten-foot radius, and it made her feel indescribably happy – more so than she remembered feeling for a very long time.

"Are you alright?" Chris asked, picking up on her sigh.

"Perfectly so," Laura said, with a smile. She reached out and touched his hand –

Chris was on one knee, fumbling with a tiny box. It was dark, the vision clouded by Zach's proximity, but Laura knew what she was looking at. He was nervous and shaking, his hands failing him for a moment, a far cry from his usual sure-handed surgeon composure. He dropped the box on the ground and swore, scrambling to get it, before finally popping it open, the diamond catching the light –

Laura ducked her head with a little smile, a little flush spreading on her cheeks before she could stop it. No headache: she didn't know how far in the future that vision was waiting for her.

"What is it?" Chris asked, trying to lean to catch her eye as she kept her head down.

"Nothing," she said, grinning and meeting his eyes again. "I'm just happy."

He brought her hand to his mouth and kissed the back of it, entwining their fingers, and she repeated it to herself in her head.

I'm just happy.

NOW AVAILABLE!

ABSENT PITY
(An Amber Young FBI Suspense Thriller—Book 1)

When Amber Young, a quiet, brilliant newspaper puzzle editor, detects a hidden cypher, she realizes a serial killer is leaving clues hidden in plain sight. The FBI's BAU unit needs Amber's unique genius to help them decode the mystery and catch a killer before it's too late, and in this page-turning, cat and mouse thriller, it's a battle of clues, riddles, twists—and genius.

"A masterpiece of thriller and mystery."
—Books and Movie Reviews, Roberto Mattos (re Once Gone)

ABSENT PITY is book #1 in a long-anticipated new series by #1 bestseller and USA Today bestselling author Blake Pierce, whose bestseller Once Gone (a free download) has received over 7,000 five star ratings and reviews.

Amber Young, shy, reclusive, prefers to avoid the limelight and quietly do her puzzle work for her newspaper. But when she finds herself at the center of a manhunt for a deadly killer, she realizes her unique genius may just mean the difference between life and death for the next victim. With a life on the line, it will require of all Amber's brilliance to outsmart a genius, diabolical killer intent on proving his smarts and taunting the FBI.

Will Amber outsmart him?

Or might she end up the next victim?

A page-turning and harrowing crime thriller featuring a brilliant and tortured FBI agent, the Amber Young series is a riveting mystery, packed with non-stop action, suspense, twists and turns, revelations, and driven by a breakneck pace that will keep you flipping pages late into the night. Fans of Rachel Caine, Teresa Driscoll and Robert Dugoni are sure to fall in love.

Future books in the series are also available.

“An edge of your seat thriller in a new series that keeps you turning pages! ...So many twists, turns and red herrings… I can't wait to see what happens next.”
—Reader review (Her Last Wish)

“A strong, complex story about two FBI agents trying to stop a serial killer. If you want an author to capture your attention and have you guessing, yet trying to put the pieces together, Pierce is your author!”
—Reader review (Her Last Wish)

“A typical Blake Pierce twisting, turning, roller coaster ride suspense thriller. Will have you turning the pages to the last sentence of the last chapter!!!”
—Reader review (City of Prey)

“Right from the start we have an unusual protagonist that I haven't seen done in this genre before. The action is nonstop… A very atmospheric novel that will keep you turning pages well into the wee hours.”
—Reader review (City of Prey)

“Everything that I look for in a book… a great plot, interesting characters, and grabs your interest right away. The book moves along at a breakneck pace and stays that way until the end. Now on go I to book two!”
—Reader review (Girl, Alone)

“Exciting, heart pounding, edge of your seat book… a must read for mystery and suspense readers!”
—Reader review (Girl, Alone)

Blake Pierce

Blake Pierce is the USA Today bestselling author of the RILEY PAGE mystery series, which includes seventeen books. Blake Pierce is also the author of the MACKENZIE WHITE mystery series, comprising fourteen books; of the AVERY BLACK mystery series, comprising six books; of the KERI LOCKE mystery series, comprising five books; of the MAKING OF RILEY PAIGE mystery series, comprising six books; of the KATE WISE mystery series, comprising seven books; of the CHLOE FINE psychological suspense mystery, comprising six books; of the JESSIE HUNT psychological suspense thriller series, comprising twenty six books; of the AU PAIR psychological suspense thriller series, comprising three books; of the ZOE PRIME mystery series, comprising six books; of the ADELE SHARP mystery series, comprising sixteen books, of the EUROPEAN VOYAGE cozy mystery series, comprising six books; of the LAURA FROST FBI suspense thriller, comprising eleven books; of the ELLA DARK FBI suspense thriller, comprising fourteen books (and counting); of the A YEAR IN EUROPE cozy mystery series, comprising nine books, of the AVA GOLD mystery series, comprising six books; of the RACHEL GIFT mystery series, comprising ten books (and counting); of the VALERIE LAW mystery series, comprising nine books (and counting); of the PAIGE KING mystery series, comprising eight books (and counting); of the MAY MOORE mystery series, comprising eleven books (and counting); the CORA SHIELDS mystery series, comprising five books (and counting); of the NICKY LYONS mystery series, comprising seven books (and counting), of the CAMI LARK mystery series, comprising five books (and counting), of the AMBER YOUNG mystery series, comprising five books (and counting), and of the new DAISY FORTUNE mystery series, comprising five books (and counting).

An avid reader and lifelong fan of the mystery and thriller genres, Blake loves to hear from you, so please feel free to visit www.blakepierceauthor.com to learn more and stay in touch.

BOOKS BY BLAKE PIERCE

DAISY FORTUNE MYSTERY SERIES

NEED YOU (Book #1)
CLAIM YOU (Book #2)
CRAVE YOU (Book #3)
CHOOSE YOU (Book #4)
CHASE YOU (Book #5)

AMBER YOUNG MYSTERY SERIES

ABSENT PITY (Book #1)
ABSENT REMORSE (Book #2)
ABSENT FEELING (Book #3)
ABSENT MERCY (Book #4)
ABSENT REASON (Book #5)

CAMI LARK MYSTERY SERIES

JUST ME (Book #1)
JUST OUTSIDE (Book #2)
JUST RIGHT (Book #3)
JUST FORGET (Book #4)
JUST ONCE (Book #5)

NICKY LYONS MYSTERY SERIES

ALL MINE (Book #1)
ALL HIS (Book #2)
ALL HE SEES (Book #3)
ALL ALONE (Book #4)
ALL FOR ONE (Book #5)
ALL HE TAKES (Book #6)
ALL FOR ME (Book #7)

CORA SHIELDS MYSTERY SERIES

UNDONE (Book #1)
UNWANTED (Book #2)
UNHINGED (Book #3)
UNSAID (Book #4)
UNGLUED (Book #5)

MAY MOORE SUSPENSE THRILLER
NEVER RUN (Book #1)
NEVER TELL (Book #2)
NEVER LIVE (Book #3)
NEVER HIDE (Book #4)
NEVER FORGIVE (Book #5)
NEVER AGAIN (Book #6)
NEVER LOOK BACK (Book #7)
NEVER FORGET (Book #8)
NEVER LET GO (Book #9)
NEVER PRETEND (Book #10)
NEVER HESITATE (Book #11)

PAIGE KING MYSTERY SERIES
THE GIRL HE PINED (Book #1)
THE GIRL HE CHOSE (Book #2)
THE GIRL HE TOOK (Book #3)
THE GIRL HE WISHED (Book #4)
THE GIRL HE CROWNED (Book #5)
THE GIRL HE WATCHED (Book #6)
THE GIRL HE WANTED (Book #7)
THE GIRL HE CLAIMED (Book #8)

VALERIE LAW MYSTERY SERIES
NO MERCY (Book #1)
NO PITY (Book #2)
NO FEAR (Book #3)
NO SLEEP (Book #4)
NO QUARTER (Book #5)
NO CHANCE (Book #6)
NO REFUGE (Book #7)
NO GRACE (Book #8)
NO ESCAPE (Book #9)

RACHEL GIFT MYSTERY SERIES
HER LAST WISH (Book #1)
HER LAST CHANCE (Book #2)
HER LAST HOPE (Book #3)
HER LAST FEAR (Book #4)

HER LAST CHOICE (Book #5)
HER LAST BREATH (Book #6)
HER LAST MISTAKE (Book #7)
HER LAST DESIRE (Book #8)
HER LAST REGRET (Book #9)
HER LAST HOUR (Book #10)

AVA GOLD MYSTERY SERIES
CITY OF PREY (Book #1)
CITY OF FEAR (Book #2)
CITY OF BONES (Book #3)
CITY OF GHOSTS (Book #4)
CITY OF DEATH (Book #5)
CITY OF VICE (Book #6)

A YEAR IN EUROPE
A MURDER IN PARIS (Book #1)
DEATH IN FLORENCE (Book #2)
VENGEANCE IN VIENNA (Book #3)
A FATALITY IN SPAIN (Book #4)

ELLA DARK FBI SUSPENSE THRILLER
GIRL, ALONE (Book #1)
GIRL, TAKEN (Book #2)
GIRL, HUNTED (Book #3)
GIRL, SILENCED (Book #4)
GIRL, VANISHED (Book 5)
GIRL ERASED (Book #6)
GIRL, FORSAKEN (Book #7)
GIRL, TRAPPED (Book #8)
GIRL, EXPENDABLE (Book #9)
GIRL, ESCAPED (Book #10)
GIRL, HIS (Book #11)
GIRL, LURED (Book #12)
GIRL, MISSING (Book #13)
GIRL, UNKNOWN (Book #14)

LAURA FROST FBI SUSPENSE THRILLER
ALREADY GONE (Book #1)
ALREADY SEEN (Book #2)

ALREADY TRAPPED (Book #3)
ALREADY MISSING (Book #4)
ALREADY DEAD (Book #5)
ALREADY TAKEN (Book #6)
ALREADY CHOSEN (Book #7)
ALREADY LOST (Book #8)
ALREADY HIS (Book #9)
ALREADY LURED (Book #10)
ALREADY COLD (Book #11)

EUROPEAN VOYAGE COZY MYSTERY SERIES
MURDER (AND BAKLAVA) (Book #1)
DEATH (AND APPLE STRUDEL) (Book #2)
CRIME (AND LAGER) (Book #3)
MISFORTUNE (AND GOUDA) (Book #4)
CALAMITY (AND A DANISH) (Book #5)
MAYHEM (AND HERRING) (Book #6)

ADELE SHARP MYSTERY SERIES
LEFT TO DIE (Book #1)
LEFT TO RUN (Book #2)
LEFT TO HIDE (Book #3)
LEFT TO KILL (Book #4)
LEFT TO MURDER (Book #5)
LEFT TO ENVY (Book #6)
LEFT TO LAPSE (Book #7)
LEFT TO VANISH (Book #8)
LEFT TO HUNT (Book #9)
LEFT TO FEAR (Book #10)
LEFT TO PREY (Book #11)
LEFT TO LURE (Book #12)
LEFT TO CRAVE (Book #13)
LEFT TO LOATHE (Book #14)
LEFT TO HARM (Book #15)
LEFT TO RUIN (Book #16)

THE AU PAIR SERIES
ALMOST GONE (Book#1)
ALMOST LOST (Book #2)
ALMOST DEAD (Book #3)

ZOE PRIME MYSTERY SERIES
FACE OF DEATH (Book#1)
FACE OF MURDER (Book #2)
FACE OF FEAR (Book #3)
FACE OF MADNESS (Book #4)
FACE OF FURY (Book #5)
FACE OF DARKNESS (Book #6)

A JESSIE HUNT PSYCHOLOGICAL SUSPENSE SERIES
THE PERFECT WIFE (Book #1)
THE PERFECT BLOCK (Book #2)
THE PERFECT HOUSE (Book #3)
THE PERFECT SMILE (Book #4)
THE PERFECT LIE (Book #5)
THE PERFECT LOOK (Book #6)
THE PERFECT AFFAIR (Book #7)
THE PERFECT ALIBI (Book #8)
THE PERFECT NEIGHBOR (Book #9)
THE PERFECT DISGUISE (Book #10)
THE PERFECT SECRET (Book #11)
THE PERFECT FAÇADE (Book #12)
THE PERFECT IMPRESSION (Book #13)
THE PERFECT DECEIT (Book #14)
THE PERFECT MISTRESS (Book #15)
THE PERFECT IMAGE (Book #16)
THE PERFECT VEIL (Book #17)
THE PERFECT INDISCRETION (Book #18)
THE PERFECT RUMOR (Book #19)
THE PERFECT COUPLE (Book #20)
THE PERFECT MURDER (Book #21)
THE PERFECT HUSBAND (Book #22)
THE PERFECT SCANDAL (Book #23)
THE PERFECT MASK (Book #24)
THE PERFECT RUSE (Book #25)
THE PERFECT VENEER (Book #26)

CHLOE FINE PSYCHOLOGICAL SUSPENSE SERIES
NEXT DOOR (Book #1)
A NEIGHBOR'S LIE (Book #2)

CUL DE SAC (Book #3)
SILENT NEIGHBOR (Book #4)
HOMECOMING (Book #5)
TINTED WINDOWS (Book #6)

KATE WISE MYSTERY SERIES
IF SHE KNEW (Book #1)
IF SHE SAW (Book #2)
IF SHE RAN (Book #3)
IF SHE HID (Book #4)
IF SHE FLED (Book #5)
IF SHE FEARED (Book #6)
IF SHE HEARD (Book #7)

THE MAKING OF RILEY PAIGE SERIES
WATCHING (Book #1)
WAITING (Book #2)
LURING (Book #3)
TAKING (Book #4)
STALKING (Book #5)
KILLING (Book #6)

RILEY PAIGE MYSTERY SERIES
ONCE GONE (Book #1)
ONCE TAKEN (Book #2)
ONCE CRAVED (Book #3)
ONCE LURED (Book #4)
ONCE HUNTED (Book #5)
ONCE PINED (Book #6)
ONCE FORSAKEN (Book #7)
ONCE COLD (Book #8)
ONCE STALKED (Book #9)
ONCE LOST (Book #10)
ONCE BURIED (Book #11)
ONCE BOUND (Book #12)
ONCE TRAPPED (Book #13)
ONCE DORMANT (Book #14)
ONCE SHUNNED (Book #15)
ONCE MISSED (Book #16)
ONCE CHOSEN (Book #17)

MACKENZIE WHITE MYSTERY SERIES
BEFORE HE KILLS (Book #1)
BEFORE HE SEES (Book #2)
BEFORE HE COVETS (Book #3)
BEFORE HE TAKES (Book #4)
BEFORE HE NEEDS (Book #5)
BEFORE HE FEELS (Book #6)
BEFORE HE SINS (Book #7)
BEFORE HE HUNTS (Book #8)
BEFORE HE PREYS (Book #9)
BEFORE HE LONGS (Book #10)
BEFORE HE LAPSES (Book #11)
BEFORE HE ENVIES (Book #12)
BEFORE HE STALKS (Book #13)
BEFORE HE HARMS (Book #14)

AVERY BLACK MYSTERY SERIES
CAUSE TO KILL (Book #1)
CAUSE TO RUN (Book #2)
CAUSE TO HIDE (Book #3)
CAUSE TO FEAR (Book #4)
CAUSE TO SAVE (Book #5)
CAUSE TO DREAD (Book #6)

KERI LOCKE MYSTERY SERIES
A TRACE OF DEATH (Book #1)
A TRACE OF MURDER (Book #2)
A TRACE OF VICE (Book #3)
A TRACE OF CRIME (Book #4)
A TRACE OF HOPE (Book #5)

Made in United States
North Haven, CT
06 January 2023